CHILD OF AN ANCIENT CITY

Books in the Dragonflight Series

CHILD OF AN ANCIENT CITY

TAD WILLIAMS
NINA KIRIKI HOFFMAN

Illustrated by
Greg Hildebrandt

A Byron Preiss Book

Atheneum 1992 New York
Maxwell Macmillan Canada
Toronto

Maxwell Macmillan International
New York   Oxford   Singapore   Sydney

CHILD OF AN ANCIENT CITY
Dragonflight Books

Copyright © 1992 by Byron Preiss Visual Publications, Inc.

Text copyright © 1992 by Tad Williams and Nina Kiriki Hoffman

Illustrations copyright © 1992 by Greg Hildebrandt

Cover painting by Greg Hildebrandt
Book design by Dean Motter
Edited by John Betancourt

Atheneum
Macmillan Publishing Company
866 Third Avenue, New York, NY 10022

Maxwell Macmillan Canada, Inc.
1200 Eglinton Avenue East
Suite 200
Don Mills, Ontario M3C 3N1

Macmillan Publishing Company is part of the Maxwell
Communication Group of Companies.

First Edition
Printed in the United States of America
10 9 8 7 6 5 4 3 2 1

Library of Congress Catalog Card Number: 92–16802

ISBN 0–689–31577–5

To Sir Richard Burton

PROLOGUE

"Merciful Allah! I am a calf, fatted for slaughter!"

Masrur al-Adan roared with laughter and crashed his goblet down on the polished wood table—once, twice, thrice. A trail of crescent-shaped dents followed his hand. "I can scarce move for gorging."

The fire was banked and shadows walked the walls. Masrur's table—for he was master here—stood scatter-spread with the bones of small fowl.

Masrur leaned forward and squinted across the table. "A calf," he said. "Fatted." He belched absently and wiped his mouth with a wine-stained sleeve.

Ibn Fahad allowed himself a thin, cold smile. "We have indeed wreaked massacre on the race of pigeons, old friend." His slim hand swept above the littered tabletop. "My compliments to your cook."

"My cook," said Masrur. He smirked. "A jewel, as well you know. However, he does not stir from the kitchen these days; his old wound still pains him. I will convey your appreciation tomorrow."

Ibn Fahad said, "We have also put the elite guard of your wine cellars to flight. And, as usual, I thank you for your hospitality. But do you not sometimes wonder if there is more to life than growing fat in the service of the Caliph?"

"Hah!" Masrur goggled his eyes. "Doing the Caliph's bidding has made me wealthy. I have made *myself* fat." He smiled. The other guests laughed and whispered.

Abu Jamir, a fatter man in an equally stained robe, toppled a small tower erected from the bones of squab. "The night is young, good Masrur!" he cried. "Have someone fetch up more wine and let us hear some stories!"

"Baba!" Masrur bellowed. "Come here, you old dog!"

Within three breaths an old servant stood in the doorway, looking to his sportive master with apprehension.

"Bring us the rest of the wine, Baba—or have you drunk it all?"

Baba pulled at a grizzled chin. "Ah . . . ah, but *you* drank it, Master. You and Master Ibn

Fahad took the last four jars with you when you went to shoot arrows from the city walls."

"Just as I suspected," Masrur nodded. "Well, get on across the bazaar to Abu Jamir's place, wake up his manservant, and bring back several jugs. The good Jamir says we must have it now."

Baba disappeared. The chagrined Abu Jamir was cheerfully back-thumped by the other guests.

"A story, a story!" someone shouted. "A tale!"

"Oh, yes, a tale of your travels, Master Masrur!" This was young Hassan, who was sinfully drunk. No one minded. His eyes were bright, and he was full of innocent stupidity. "Someone said you have traveled to the green lands of the north."

"The north . . . ?" Masrur grumbled, waving his hand as though confronted with something unclean, "No, lad, no . . . that I cannot give to you." His face clouded and he slumped back on his cushions; his tarbooshed head swayed.

Ibn Fahad knew his old comrade Masrur like he knew his horses—indeed, the large fellow was the only human that could claim so much of Ibn Fahad's attention. He had seen Masrur drink twice the quantity he had downed tonight and still dance like a dervish on the walls of Baghdad, but Ibn Fahad thought he could guess the reason for this sudden incapacity.

"Oh, Masrur, please!" Hassan had not given

3

up; he was as unshakeable as a young falcon with its first prey beneath its talons. "Tell us of the north. Tell us of the infidels!"

"A good Moslem should not show such interest in unbelievers." Abu Jamir sniffed piously, shaking the last drops from a wine jug. "If Masrur does not wish to tell a tale, let him be."

"Hah!" snorted the host, recovering somewhat. "You only seek to stall me, Jamir, so that my throat shall not be so dry when your wine arrives. No, I have no fear of speaking of unbelievers; Allah would not have given them a place in the world for their own if they had not *some* use. Rather it is . . . certain other things that happened which make me hesitate." He gazed kindly on young Hassan, who in the depths of his drunkenness looked likely to cry. "Do not despair, eggling. Perhaps it would do me good to unfold this story. I have kept the details long inside." He emptied the dregs of another jar into his cup. "I still feel it so strongly, though—bitter, bitter times. Why don't *you* tell the story, my good friend?" he said over his shoulder to Ibn Fahad. "You played as much a part as did I. You tell."

"No," Ibn Fahad replied. Drunken puppy Hassan emitted a strangled cry of despair.

"But why, old comrade?" Masrur asked, pivoting his bulk to stare in amazement. "Did the experience so chill even *your* heart?"

Ibn Fahad glowered. "Because I know better.

4

As soon as I start you will interrupt, adding details here, magnifying there, then saying: 'No, no, I cannot speak of it! Continue, old friend!' Before I have taken another breath you will interrupt me again. You *know* you will wind up doing all the talking, Masrur. Why do you not start from the beginning and save me my breath?"

All laughed but Masrur, who put on a look of wounded solicitousness. "Of course, old friend," he murmured. "I had no idea that you harbored such grievances. Of course I shall tell the tale." A broad wink was offered to the table. "No sacrifice is too great for a friendship such as ours. Poke up the fire, will you, Baba? Ah, he's gone. Hassan, will you be so kind?"

When the youth was again seated Masrur took a swallow, stroked his beard, and began.

Chapter 1:

THE CARAVAN

In those days [Masrur said], I myself was but a lowly soldier in the service of Harun al-Rashid, may Allah grant him peace. I was young, strong, a man who loved wine more than he should—but what soldier does not?—and a good deal more trim and comely than you see me today.

My troop received a commission to accompany a caravan going north, bound for the land of the Armenites beyond the Caucassian Mountains. A certain prince of that people had sent a great store of gifts as tribute to the Caliph, gifts of a richness no one could ignore: crowns of beaten gold with diamonds inset, daggers of a metal harder than those in the Caliph's armory, and hanks of black wool carded to a marvelous softness and spun into thread as fine as a girl-child's hair. This prince invited the Caliph to open a route for trade between his principality and our caliphate.

Harun al-Rashid, wisest of wise men that he was, did not exactly make the camels groan beneath the weight of the gifts that he sent in return, but he did send three slaves, one a master in the art of cookery, and several courtiers, including the Under-Vizier Walid al-Salameh, who had made a study of barbarian dialects and could speak for the Caliph and assure this Armenite prince that rich rewards would follow when the route over the Caucassians was opened for good.

We left Baghdad in grand style: pennants flying, the shields of the soldiers flashing like golden dinars, slaves bearing the boxed litters of the courtiers, and the Caliph's gifts bundled onto the backs of a gang of evil, contrary donkeys.

We followed the banks of the Tigris, resting and provisioning several days at Mosul, then continued through the eastern edge of Anatolia. Already as we mounted northward the land was beginning to change, the clean sands giving way to rocky hills and scrub. The weather was colder and the skies gray, as though even in the season of spring Allah's face was turned away from that country, but the men were not unhappy to be out from under the desert sun. Our pace was good; there was not a hint of danger except the occasional howls of wolves beyond the circles of our nightly campfires. Before two months had passed we had reached the foothills of the Caucassians— what is called the steppe country.

For those of you who have not strayed far from our Bagdad, I should tell you that the northern lands are like nothing you have seen. The trees there grow so close together you could not throw a stone five paces without striking one. In the foothills are nut-bearing trees with leaves smaller than your hand, clustered as thickly as the hairs in my beard, but higher in the mountains stand trees with branches bearing clumps of fragrant green needles all the way down the trunk. The land itself seems always dark—the trees mask the sun before the afternoon is properly finished—and the ground is damp, with many stones. Ravines, deeper than any minaret stands high, cleave the mountains, and water plumes and plunges over steep drop-offs like pale horses' tails. On the high peaks, of which there are many, snow clings, even in the height of summer. Indeed, we saw in one place near the top of the pass a field several leagues wide made entirely of ice.

But, in truth, the novelty of it faded quickly, and before long it seemed that the smell of decay was always with us. We caravaners had been over eight weeks traveling, and the bite of homesickness was strong, but we contented ourselves with the thought of the accommodations that would be ours when we reached the palace of the prince, laden as we were with our Caliph's good wishes— and the tangible proof thereof. I myself had never been to a northern principality before, though I had seen northern goods traded at market, and I wondered what strange new things, people, and creatures I might observe. As I said, *all* my appetites were strong in those days.

We had just crossed the high mountain passes and begun our journey down when disaster struck.

We were encamped one night in a box canyon, a thousand steep feet below the summit of the tall Caucassian peaks. The fires were not much but glowing coals, and nearly all the camp was asleep except for two men standing sentry. I was wrapped in my bedroll, dreaming of how I would spend my earnings—dreaming especially of a girl with a neck slender as a gazelle's, hair like night, and a gaze that filled my heart with longing—when a terrible shriek awakened me.

Sitting groggily upright, I was promptly knocked down by some bulky thing tumbling onto my chest. A moment's horrified examination showed that it was one of the sentries, his throat pierced with an arrow, his eyes bulging with his final surprise. Suddenly there was a chorus of howls from the hillside above. My heart pounded. All I could think of was wolves, that the wolves were coming down on us: In my witless state I could make no sense of the arrow at all.

Even as the others sprang up around me the camp was suddenly filled with leaping, whooping shadows, as though the gates of Hell had swung open to release their prisoners. The coppery scent of fresh blood tainted the air. Blades glinted in the faint light of the coals and another arrow hissed past my face in the darkness. The groans of wounded and dying men, the grunts of effort as others threw themselves into combat, the clash of blade on blade—Allah be praised, these sounds awakened sense in me, for I had been in battle before. These were human wolves we faced.

I reached for my sword's hilt, but my blade and I were both pinioned beneath the dead sentry. As I struggled to push the unfortunate man off me, a booted foot suddenly stamped the soil near my head. I lay still as just above me a bandit and one of my comrades crossed blades.

The bandit, garbed in black—as I later learned is the custom of these Caucassian rogues—bore an immense curved blade that gleamed red in the dying light. I later learned that my comrade-at-arms was only a slender youth.

(And did you not suspect, Ibn Fahad, old friend, that our mission was not of the greatest importance, since most of the soldiers with the caravan were inexperienced and unblooded? I myself had been disciplined recently for the incident with the Frankish unbeliever and the donkey, and thought this journey might have been meted out to me as part of my penance—a trip through lands where ice lay on the ground meant to cool my blood, as indeed it did—but this did not explain *your* presence, old comrade. I doubt not there's a tale in it.)

So I lay on the ground, bladeless and cursing silently. Soon enough the young soldier took a stab to the stomach and collapsed beside me, his eyes half open as they stared into the next world. I had lain still throughout, hoping to escape detection, for pinioned as I was by the sentry's corpse, I had not a hope of defense.

My deception must have been successful, for after cutting the purse off the dead soldier's belt and glancing at the sentry lying upon me, the bandit turned and hurried away.

Ah, Ibn Fahad, old friend, you laugh at my unusual discretion in that long-ago time; but even *I* know that sometimes a still tongue can preserve a life.

But, of course, under other circumstances, a quiet tongue can lead to a cut throat.

In any case, there I was in a moment of lull between assaults, protected by night-shadows. I finally succeeded in heaving off the sentry's corpse and freeing my blade from its scabbard, and I was just about to rise and join my fellows in battle.

Then something crashed against my bare head, filling the nighttime with a great splash of light that illuminated nothing.

I fell back, insensible.

Chapter 2:

AFTERMATH

I could not tell how long I had journeyed in that deeper darkness when a sharp boot prodding at my ribcage finally roused me.

I looked up at a tall, cruel figure, cast in bold outline by the cloud-curtained morning sun. As my sight became accustomed to the light I saw a knife-thin face, dark-browed and fierce, with mustachios long as a Tartar herdsman's. I felt sure that whoever had struck me had returned to finish the job, and I struggled weakly to pull my dagger from my sash. This terrifying figure merely lifted one of his pointy boots and trod delicately on my wrist, saying in perfect Arabic: "Wonders of Allah, this is the dirtiest man I have ever seen."

It was Ibn Fahad, of course. The caravan had

been of good size, and he had been riding with the Armenite and the Under-Vizier—not back with the ragtag rabble—so we had never spoken. Now you see how we first truly met: me on my back, covered with mud, blood, and spit; and Ibn Fahad standing over me like a rich man examining Afghani carrots in the bazaar. Infamy!

Ibn Fahad had been blessed with what I would come later to know as his usual luck. When the bandits—who must have been following us for some days—came down upon us in the night, Ibn Fahad had been voiding his bladder some distance away along the slope outside camp. Running back at the sound of the first cries, he had sent more than a few mountain bandits down to Hell with his swift sword, but they were too many. He had pulled together a small group of survivors from the main party and they had fought their way free, then retreated along the mountain in the darkness, listening to the screams echoing behind them and cursing their small numbers and ignorance of the country.

Coming back in the light of day to scavenge for supplies, as well as to ascertain the nature of our attackers, Ibn Fahad had found me—a fact he has never allowed me to forget, and for which *I* have never allowed *him* to evade responsibility.

While my wounds were doctored, Ibn Fahad introduced me to the few survivors of our once-great caravan.

One was Susri al-Din—a cheerful lad, fresh-faced and smooth-cheeked as our young Hassan here, dressed in the robes of a rich merchant's son. The soldiers who had survived rather liked him, and came to call him "Fawn," teasing him for his wide-eyed good looks. There was a skinny wretch of a chief clerk named Abdallah, purse-mouthed and iron-eyed, and an indecently plump young mullah, who had just left the *madrasa* and was getting a rather rude introduction to life outside the seminary. Ruad, the mullah, looked as though he would prefer to be drinking and laughing with the soldiers—beside myself and Ibn Fahad there were six more of these: Rifakh, Mohammad, Nizam, Achmed, Bekir, all young and inexperienced, and Hamed, an old campaigner whose joints were troubled by the damps of the mountains—while Abdallah the prim-faced clerk looked as though he should be the one who abstained from drink and never lifted his head out of the Koran. Well, in a way that was true, since for a man like Abdallah the balance book *is* the Holy Book, may Allah forgive such blasphemy.

Also in the company was a Turkish slave, Ibrahim, a cheery fellow, small and gnarled, with the heels of his hands stained yellow by saffron: though many of his race were slaves in the lands of Islam and highly regarded for their military prowess, Ibrahim's skills lay rather in the area of the culinary arts. Ibn Fahad, however, said

Ibrahim had proved himself ready with a dagger when needed, and had proved in the conflict with the bandits that he was able to slice throats as well as stew meat.

There was one other, notable for the extreme richness of his robes, the extreme whiteness of his beard, and the vast weight of his personal jewelry—Walid al-Salameh, the Under-Vizier to His Eminence the Caliph Harun al-Rashid. Walid was the most important man of the whole party. He was also, surprisingly, not a bad fellow at all.

So there we found ourselves, the wreck of the Caliph's embassy, with no hope but to try and find our way back home through a strange, hostile land.

The bandits had left not a single pack animal, and they had plundered all the gifts intended for the Armenite prince, which, in any case, would have been of little use to us now. Ibrahim, more familiar with the food supplies of the caravan than the rest of us, turned up a cache of desert bread, pistachio kernels, spiced dried lamb, and dried dates, for which we profusely thanked Allah. He also, with great delight, recovered his cache of precious spices. The rest of us searched among the dead for whatever weapons we could use, and contrived as best we could to gather and prepare the bodies of our comrades for burial. We had not enough water skins or strength to carry water to

17

wash them all, but we did wash their faces, and then, since we had no shrouds, covered their faces with their tunics and repeated *Allahu Akbar*. The earth in that place was hard and rocky; and so it was that instead of digging into the ground (for which work we had only swords) we laid out our dead and piled stones upon them. Ruad the mullah performed his first funeral prayers over the bodies of our comrades while Ibrahim built a fire and, as best he could from the meager supplies left to us, put together a stew for the funeral feast.

Our work had taken us most of the day. In truth, I was relieved to be able to sit down with a bowl of fragrant stew, even though it was a feast for the dead; even though I had laid out bodies of men I had played cards with and caroused with, men with whom I had shared jokes and quarrels. I had not a chance to eat much, though, when the bandits, wailing like angry demons, returned.

Chapter 3:
LOST

We were too woefully few to face the well-armed and well-mounted bandits. Fortunately, we had packed all the supplies we had found before we attended to the burial, so we were ready to flee— or as ready as any men could be who would rather stand and fight. This time we were not distracted by fancies of what the fearsome noises in the night might be; indeed, I had to drag Rifakh after us, for he had drawn his sword and stood ready to attack. Fawn also showed an inclination to remain and be cut down, but the Under-Vizier persuaded him to join in our rout.

This was home ground to the wicked Caucassians, but they were hampered by the unfamiliarity of their horses (one of which I recognized as the steed the Armenite ambassador had ridden). Ibn Fahad, who was leading us, headed for the thickest part of the nearby woods, a tactic which proved useful indeed. In the perpetual twilight beneath the trees, soon joined by actual night, we managed to evade the looters, although we lost ourselves and each other in the process.

I did not at that time know about Ibn Fahad's luck. During the preparations for burial of the dead I had not taken particular notice of him, aside from offering Allah thanks for his and the other survivors' return to the battlefield. That night, as I lost track of the others in our party and at last stumbled to rest beneath a fallen tree, listening to the quiet footfalls of beasts around me and wondering what strange animals might walk in this northern wilderness, I had time to think. Although the Under-Vizier Walid al-Salameh had the highest rank of any of us, I recalled that it was Ibn Fahad who had suggested we pack our supplies before attending to the dead, and it was Ibn Fahad who had led our retreat. Here was a man with more military experience than I had, and furthermore, a man who thought well in the midst of things.

(Hah! See, my guests, even now Ibn Fahad pretends to snore; overt praises bore him.) In any case, I resolved that if I should find him and the others again, I would pay him particular mind. (Hmm. If he were awake he would certainly laugh to hear me say that, so he *must* be sleeping.)

Morning light brought me strength of heart. In the distance I heard the musical trickle of water, echoing strangely through the mist that concealed the treetops and the distances. Chilled and damp, I crept from my shelter and sought for the stream, not only for my morning ablutions but to slake the thirst burning in my throat.

Fortune was with me. At a small rocky rill I came face-to-face with Ibn Fahad and the slave Ibrahim, stooping to fill waterskins. "The last of our wandering sheep returns," Ibn Fahad observed upon seeing me. He had sniffed out the others in our party before dawn and gathered them in a clearing. Following him and the Turk, I rejoined the company and shared the scanty breakfast, thankful again to be alive and unalone.

The upper reaches of the Caucassians are a cold and Godless place. The fog is thick and wet; it crawls in with the morning, leaves briefly at the time the sun is high, then comes creeping back long before sunset. We were sodden as well-diggers from the moment we stepped into the foothills. A treacherous place, those mountains: filled with bear and wolf, covered in forest so thick that in places the sun was lost completely.

We had run far in our flight from the bandits, and none of us had marked our direction in the darkness. Since we had no guide—indeed, it was several days before we saw any sign of inhabitants whatsoever—we wandered lost, losing half as much ground as we gained for walking in circles.

At last we were forced to admit our need for a trained local eye. In the middle slopes the trees grew so thick that fixing our direction was impossible for hours at a time. We were divining the location of Mecca by general discussion and—blasphemy again!—we probably spent as much time praying toward Aleppo as we did toward the Holy of Holies. (Our mullah had no better idea of which direction to aim our prayers than the rest of us.) In short, we faced a hard choice between possible discovery and certain doom.

In the night we had smelled the smoke of wood fires other than our own, and sometimes the scent of food cooking. Once on a clear night we had even seen the lights of a mountain village twinkling in the twilight, but in our wary state we had veered away from any contact with these mountain people. Who knew what welcome they would give us?

Those we had glimpsed by day seemed a clannish bunch, not given to wandering off alone. Some, men and women both, drove animals into the high peaks to summer pasturelands, where they watched herds of goats and sheep but always remained within call of one another.

Ruad the mullah suggested one of us approach a settlement and ask for a guide. Abdallah the clerk sneered at such a suggestion: "How could we pay?

Would we not be revealing to them our existence and our defenselessness?" he asked, and though I did not wish to side with the clerk, I felt his argument had merit. "How can we expect charity of infidels?" Abdallah added.

That day the sun showed itself early enough for us to determine which direction was south, and to pursue it; so we did not resolve the argument, save perhaps by the fact that we chanced upon another settlement, a tight cluster of small squatting wooden buildings huddled against the side of a hill, and we immediately headed west away from it.

In the cool gray early morning of the following day, we came across a strange stone shelter on a high crag, almost above the treeline. It was as small as a nomad's tent, and did not look as though it could shelter more than four people at once. The stones were dressed without mortar or plaster to form two walls and a roof extending out from the mountain, but one end of this curious structure stood open, and a stream trickled forth from there.

Achmed and I separated from the rest of our party and crept closer. Within the shelter lay a small, still-surfaced pool ringed with large flat stones. On one of these stones a youth knelt, staring at the quiet water as if entranced, a wilting bunch of late spring flowers under his hand. He did not appear to have heard our approach, which was, because of the welcome we had already received from other of the local inhabitants, stealthy. Achmed slipped up behind him and grasped the youth's shoulders. The boy startled, a low cry escaping him, and when he beheld us, his face drained of blood.

Chapter 4:

NIGHT NOISES

I felt sorry for the young peasant-lout we'd kidnapped. In a way, I still do, since our coming altered his life completely and permanently, but it was obviously the will of Allah. In any case, once this young rustic—his name, we later discovered, was Kurken, an ugly sound with no meaning behind it, unpleasant on civilized tongues—realized that we were not ghosts or Jinni, and were *not* going to kill him on the spot, he calmed down and became quite useful.

Among these mountains that cleave out separate fields of sky, languages vary from one valley to the next. People in good standing in their own villages do not leave their homes and have scant need to learn other tongues; but here was where we hit another stroke of fortune, for this lad had a little traveling under his sash and thus knew not only landmarks, but a bit of Arabic, which pious mullahs have sometimes brought into the hills in service to Allah, preaching the words of the Prophet in the town squares of tiny villages, sometimes in the very face of the Christian churches. (Christians, though infidels, are people of the Book. Some, when listening to the wisdom of the Koran, may learn the difference between good and evil and convert to the one true faith. And whether or not they convert, some do learn to converse.)

With the help of his few words, and with the Under-Vizier's small but useful knowledge of Caucassian speech, we were able to communicate with the lad.

Fawn asked the youth what he had been doing at the sheltered pond. At first he pretended to misunderstand the question, but we could tell by the sudden red in his cheeks that there was more to it.

"Let us not tease him about it," cautioned the Under-Vizier. "We have no need of this secret; I do not believe it will carry us any closer to home."

We then asked something dearer to our purposes, the cardinal points of the compass, and the boy readily supplied us with this knowledge. When he learned that our destination lay in the south, he became uneasy again, glancing that direction and shaking his head.

"Don't be alarmed," said Bekir, a young soldier whose beard scarcely covered his chin. "We have swords and we have knowledge."

"That is why we skulk about these crags like palm rats away from their trees," Ibn Fahad said, nodding sagely.

"I can lead you east—Tbilisi," said the youth in his stumbling Arabic. "From there you can find a caravan, take you home."

"We will go south," said the Under-Vizier Walid al-Salameh, in a voice of pronouncement that would admit no denial. Like all of us, I am sure, he longed to see sand beneath the sun, to be out from under the soaks and ill humors of this wet air as quickly as possible.

Kurken protested—rather strongly for someone who was, after all, our prisoner—but we overbore him and headed south, carrying him along with us, for he had methods of divination of direction which we did not know.

Under Walid's tutelege, the boy's skill with our tongue increased steadily. I exchanged a few words with him, questioning him especially about fighting methods employed by his people, but he hailed from a clan-tradition other than that of the bandits who had attacked us; he did not understand sword fighting at all.

With Kurken's aid, we began to make real progress, reaching the peak of the nearest ridge in two days.

27

There was a slight feeling of celebration in the air that night, our first in days under the open skies. Ibrahim had contrived to capture several fish in a pool we had rested beside near the end of the day's march, and he was delighted to have something fresh to prepare for us. The smell of it cooking cheered us all. The soldiers, unawed by the young mullah, cursed the lack of strong drink, but still we were happier than we'd been for a long time.

As the Under-Vizier Walid told a humorous story, I looked about the camp. There were but two grim faces: the clerk Abdallah—which was to be expected, since he seemed a patently sour old devil—and the stolen peasant-boy. I walked over to Kurken.

"Ho, young one," I said, "why do you look so downcast? Have you not realized that we are good-hearted, God-fearing men, and will not harm you?"

He did not even raise his chin, which rested shepherd-style on his knees, but he turned his eyes up to mine.

"It is not those things," he said. "It is not you soldiers but . . . this place."

"Gloomy mountains they are indeed," I agreed, "but why should it bother you? You have lived here all your young life."

"Not this place. We never come here—it is unholy. Vampyr walks these peaks."

"*Vampyr?*" said I. "And what peasant-devil is that?"

He would say no more, no matter how I coaxed, but he appeared more frightened than angry; I left him to his brooding and walked back to the fire.

When I related Kurken's words, the men all had a good laugh over the vampyr, making jesting guesses as to what type of beast it might be, but the mullah, Ruad, waved his hands urgently.

"I have heard of these ifrits," he said. "They are not to be laughed at by such a Godless lot as yourselves."

He said this as a sort of scolding joke, but he wore a strange look on his round face; we listened with interest as he continued.

"The vampyr is a restless spirit. It is neither alive nor dead, and Shaitan possesses its soul utterly. It sleeps in a sepulcher by day, and when the moon rises it goes out to feed upon travelers, to drink their blood."

Some of the men again laughed loudly, but this time it rang false as a brass-merchant's smile.

"I have heard of these from one of our foreign visitors," said the Under-Vizier Walid quietly. "He told me of a plague of these *vampyri* in a village near Smyrna. All the inhabitants fled, and the village is still uninhabited today."

This reminded someone else of a tale about an ifrit with teeth growing on both sides of his head. Others followed with their own demon stories. The talk went on late into the night and no one left the campfire until it had completely burned out.

The following morning we were somewhat the worse for our late night, but we stumbled on, cheerful in the knowledge that at least we were heading in the right direction. It was only as evening dark settled over the mountains like a black hen brooding on strange sharp eggs that the uneasiness we had felt the night before returned.

At dusk the soldier Mohammad shot a deer with one of the arrows we had scavenged from the caravan battlefield, so again we had fresh meat. Ibrahim had salt, cinnamon, and cloves in the spice cache he carried, which added savor to our evening meal. When we had all eaten enough to fill us for the first time since the bandit attack, and were sitting beside the fire in a pleasant stupor, I glanced at the peasant boy. He sat near the outer edge of the firelight, facing half away from it, his shoulders hunched, his face alert. (Earlier in the day, while we were momentarily behind the others, Ibn Fahad and I had shared our concern that perhaps this lad would scamper off. We had agreed, however, that he would probably not go at night, when proximity to our party and the fire protected him from this mountain devil he feared; daylight, when his devil lay still, would be the time he would make his attempt. So, during the day, Ibn Fahad and I took turns keeping an eye on him, seeing that he did not wander away altogether.)

But now, watching the peasant lad Kurken, I was still uneasy. I could not claim to understand the customs of these mountain unbelievers. Perhaps he had a charm to protect him from the devil. So, as I listened to Fawn telling the tale of the porter and the three ladies of Baghdad—a tale so rich in frolic it was surprising one so young knew it—I kept half an eye on the Armenite boy.

Presently I saw him stiffen, straightening. He turned toward the outer darkness of the forest. His head moved with quick short movements as his eyes sought something unseen. An instant later he was on his feet, crouching, one hand on the ground, and I was afraid that if he sprinted off into the night we would never recover him. I rose also, and heard—as Fawn broke off his tale in response to my action—a distinct sound of twigs breaking. The others leapt up, drawing swords and daggers.

For a moment we all stood frozen. The night was heavy with silence eased only by the crackling of the flames. At last the soldier Nizan called out, "Who goes there?" A shiver crept up my spine. All the night-devils from the previous evening's tale-telling returned to haunt me as I waited for a reply from the darkness.

"*Bismillah,*" said Ruad, softly. "Allah Almighty."

There was another crackling of twigs, then a dark shape stepped out of the forest into the firelight.

Chapter 5:
OUT OF THE DARKNESS

A thousand dark fancies filled my brain. The flickering shadow the creature threw against the trees seemed heavy with evil intent. I thought of all the things I had left undone, all the pleasures I had never sampled. Then the thing stepped closer to the firelight.

Here was not the tall, dark, looming figure of a jinn or ifrit, nor the soul-chilling blood-drinking thing Ruad had described, but rather a somewhat mournful, small, slender figure in boots, baggy pants, and a long dark jacket with many small buttons; its head was wrapped several times around in a striped scarf. A pack hung at its side, sadly flat. It stared at us with large defiant dark eyes, arms crossed.

"*Sossi!*" said the Armenite boy, an explosive burst of sound.

"Kurken," replied the stranger in a light musical voice.

"A female, by Allah," murmured Ibn Fahad, who stood near me.

I blinked and saw he perceived aright. She looked little more than a child, and indeed she wore no veil on her face. Still, there was something in her eyes and walk that suggested womanhood. Among all the strange creatures I had feared would emerge from the forest, one such as this had never entered my mind.

"Sossi," said the youth again, then burst into a torrent of his native tongue. It was clear from his tone that he was berating her.

I moved to stand beside Walid al-Salameh. In an undertone, he translated as best he could what the boy was saying: He demanded to know why she would risk her life coming here, where everyone knew terrible death, the vampyr, lurked in the night? How could she be so stupid? How could she throw herself away when he survived among these foreign devils only by comforting himself with the thought that no matter what happened to him she would remain safe? Now they were both doomed, and there was nothing he could do to save her.

I must say the lad's conviction, expressed so forcefully—even though in a language I did not speak—convinced me where his earlier apprehensions had not: He truly believed that this was haunted ground, that there was no escape, that we were all doomed. His voice shook with fear and anger; its sound chilled my blood.

She stood silent under this flood of words. Once, an eyebrow lifted. Once, her lips narrowed a little. In the end, she shrugged and stepped closer to the fire, her eyes on the last bony remnants of our feast. The boy was still talking to her, but she had turned her back to him. Arms crossed, she stared at Ibrahim the cook, then glanced at the leavings.

He gave her the smile with which he greeted all hungry people: He considered such folk gifts from Allah, opportunities for him to practice his craft. With his characteristic cheer and generosity, he sliced off a hunk of meat and offered it to her, and finally her arms came uncrossed as she accepted it. She ducked her head and uttered a word I took to be thanks. Then she sat, tailor-fashion, and ate, in the manner of unbelievers everywhere, using both hands to hold her food, biting it off, swallowing each mouthful almost without chewing. These people must be part wolf, I thought.

The Armenite boy advanced upon her, his face set in an angry grimace, and he continued to revile her, until Walid al-Salameh the Under-Vizier said, "*Bass.* Enough. This person is known to you?"

The lad sat down, his face pale. "Yes," he said.

"A relative?" suggested Ruad the mullah.

"No."

"A loved one?" Fawn ventured.

Kurken stared at the earth with downcast eyes and said naught for the space of six breaths. At last he unburdened himself of a deep sigh and looked up again. He tried to begin in Arabic, then switched to his own language, which the Under-Vizier struggled to translate. "She has brought herself here, into the heart of danger," he said. "She, the unattainable, the jewel of my heart." He glanced around our circle, seeing that he held all of our interest. With the aid of the Under-Vizier, Kurken told us the following tale:

"I do not know how these things are arranged in the lowlands, but here in the mountains marriages are usually decided by one's parents or god-parents. Or sometimes, as with me, my father and his friend decided when I was born and the friend's daughter was born that we were to be betrothed. This union would have left both of our families richer. I grew up believing that the girl Arpine and I would marry—until the day I passed the village fountain and saw Sossi there with water jars."

At this he fell silent, and stared into the fire for a while. The girl, Sossi, had been watching him as he talked, though she continued to eat. He frowned at the fire, then glanced at the girl. "Sossi and I are only separated by six navels, and church law forbids us to marry—"

Abdallah snorted. "What means this, 'six navels'?" he demanded. The Under-Vizier asked the boy for clarification.

When the boy responded, Walid made him repeat what he said slowly, and translated as he went: "She is my father's mother's father's sister's son's daughter's daughter."

"A serious matter, indeed," said Ibn Fahad.

Understanding, the boy flushed under this gentle sarcasm. "It was wrong for me to desire her, and for her to desire me. It was wrong for us to meet in secret and even to talk. It was most of all wrong for me to go to the spring sacred to Anahit and ask the goddess's help in this matter, for I am a good Christian, and that was a heathen thing to do. And I have been answered by being captured by you people and brought to this place of doom. I did not think my evil would drag Sossi here with me, though."

"It appears she has brought herself here," said Ibn Fahad, and smiled at the girl, who quickly cast her gaze down.

It was not easy to understand Kurken's overwhelming attraction, and it did not speak well of the girl he had spurned for this Sossi. The woman-child before us was a creature almost entirely free of the arts of attraction, wearing no scent but her own, devoid of any artful facial coloring, lacking even the kind mysteries of veils or other flatteringly concealing clothing. Nor had she any of the demure respectability of the women of our race; she seemed brazen and shameless as a boy. That she had followed Kurken into this wilderness where dwelt devils of peasant imagination bespoke either great devotion or immense foolishness, possibly both.

In any case, she was clearly frightened to be in the midst of strangers. I thought it a pity he had proffered her such a rude greeting, so I said, "However it chances, here she is, and very young too. Surely she is one of the poor the Prophet enjoins us to care for, for all she possesses is herself and her pack. Let us lay up store in Paradise by caring for her here on Earth."

Ruad the mullah seconded my motion, and none gainsaid it, though Abdallah frowned mightily, as if he thought the girl might bring us ill luck. Among my possessions I had an extra *taylasan*, a length of wide black fabric, which I offered her. For a moment she looked at it, then scrubbed her hands on her trousers and held them out, palms up. Her eyelids were lowered so that her lashes concealed her eyes, as if she were afraid to look into my face. I placed the *taylasan* across her hands. She murmured something full of hard consonants and broad vowels, bobbed her head once, then wrapped the cloth around herself, curling up in the process so that she ended up resembling a small round black rock near the fire.

I took this as a fitting indication that it was time to retire for the night. Leaving Achmed to walk sentry, the rest of us made our obeisance toward Mecca and prepared for sleep.

By noon the next day we had left the heights and were passing back down into the dark, tree-blanketed ravines. Kurken and Sossi were both quiet and untroublesome, and we covered a great deal of ground. When we stopped that night we were once more hidden from the stars, out of sight of Allah and the sky.

I remember waking up in the foredawn hours. My beard was wet with dew, and I was damnably tangled up in my cloak. A great, dark shape stood over me. I must confess to making a bit of a squawking noise.

"It's me," the shape hissed—it was Rifakh, one of the soldiers.

"You gave me a turn."

Rifakh chuckled. "Thought I was that vampyr, eh? Sorry. Just stepping out to relieve myself." He stepped over me, and I heard him trampling the underbrush. I slipped back into sleep.

The sun was just barely over the horizon when I was again awakened, this time by Ibn

Fahad tugging at my arm. I grumbled at him to leave me alone, but he had a grip on me like an alms-beggar.

"Rifakh's gone," he said. "Wake up. Have you seen him?"

"He walked on me in the middle of the night, on his way to go moisten a tree," I said. "He probably fell in the darkness and hit his head on something—have you looked?"

"Several times," Ibn Fahad responded. "All around the camp. No sign of him. Did he say anything to you?"

"Nothing interesting. Perhaps he has met the *seventh*-navel cousin of our peasant-boy, and is off somewhere making the two-backed beast."

Ibn Fahad showed a sour face at my crudity. "Perhaps not. Perhaps he has met some *other* beast."

"Don't worry," I said. "If he hasn't fallen down somewhere close by, he'll be back."

But he did not come back. When the rest of our party arose we had another long search, with no result. Tracking has never been a skill I lay claim to, and though I tried to show Bekir—the closest thing we had to a wild Bedouin in our party, thus most likely to know signs—the place where Rifakh had stumbled off into darkness, he found a few mashed twigs and then nothing. At noon we decided, reluctantly, to go on our way,

40

hoping that if he had strayed somewhere he could catch up with us.

We hiked down into the valley, going farther and farther into the trees. There was no sign of Rifakh, although from time to time we stopped and shouted in case he was searching for us. We felt there was small risk of discovery by hostile locals, for that dark valley was as empty as a pauper's purse; nevertheless, after a while the sound of our voices echoing back through the damp glades became unpleasant and we continued on in silence.

Twilight comes early in the bosom of the mountains; by midafternoon it was already turning dark. Young Fawn—the nickname had well and truly stuck, against the youth's protests—who of all of us was the most disturbed by the disappearance of Rifakh, stopped the company suddenly, shouting: "Look there!"

We turned to see where he was pointing, but the thick trees and shadows revealed nothing.

"I saw a shape!" the young one said. "It was just a short way back, following us. Perhaps it is the missing soldier."

Naturally the men ran back to look, but though we scoured the bushes we could find no trace of anyone. We decided that the failing light had played Fawn a trick—that he had seen a hind or something similar.

Two other times he called out that he saw a

shape. The last time one of the other soldiers glimpsed it too: a dark, manlike form, moving rapidly beneath the trees a bow-shot away. Close inspection still yielded no evidence, and as the group trod wearily back to the path again, Walid the Under-Vizier turned to Fawn with a hard, flat look.

"Perhaps it would be better, young master, if you talked no more of shadow-shapes."

"But I saw it!" the boy cried. "That soldier Mohammad saw it too!"

"I have no doubt of that," answered Walid al-Salameh, "but think on this: We have gone several times to see what it might be, and have found no sign of any living man. Perhaps our Rifakh is dead—perhaps he fell into a stream and drowned, or hit his head upon a rock. His spirit may be following us because it does not wish to stay in this unfamiliar place. That does not mean we want to go and find it."

"But . . ." the other began.

"Enough!" spat the chief clerk Abdallah. "You heard the Under-Vizier, young prankster. We shall have no more talk of your Godless spirits. You will straightaway leave off telling such things!"

"Your concern is appreciated, Abdallah," Walid said coldly, "but I do not require your help in this matter." The Under-Vizier strode away.

I was almost glad the clerk had added his voice, because the spreading of such frightening ideas would not keep the journey in good order . . . but, like the Under-Vizier, I too had been rubbed and grated by the clerk's high-handedness. I am sure others felt the same, for no more was said on the subject all evening.

Allah, though, always has the last word—and who are *we* to try to understand His ways? We bedded down a very quiet camp that night, the idea of poor Rifakh's lost soul hanging unspoken in the air.

From a thin, unpleasant sleep I woke to find the camp in chaos. "It's Mohammad!" Fawn was crying. "He's been killed! He's dead!"

It was true. The mullah Ruad, first up in the morning, had found the man's blanket empty, then found his body a few short yards out of the clearing.

"His throat has been slashed out," said Ibn Fahad.

It looked like a wild beast had been at him. His face was paler than it had ever been in life. His eyes were wide open, the whites visible all the way around. The ground beneath him bore only a few drops of blood. Above the cursing of the soldiers and the murmured holy words of the mullah, who looked quite green of face, I heard another sound. The young Armenite lad, grimly silent all the day before, was rocking back and forth on the ground by the remains of the cook-fire, moaning.

"Vampyr . . ." he wept, ". . . vampyr, the vampyr . . ."

The girl Sossi had veiled herself in the *taylasan* I had given her; only her eyes showed above the black cloth. She sat close beside Kurken and studied her chosen one in silence. At last she put her hand on his back, but he did not seem to notice.

All the companions were, of course, completely unmanned by these events. While we buried Mohammad in a hastily dug grave, those assembled darted glances over their shoulders into the forest vegetation. Even Ruad, as he spoke the words of the holy Koran, had trouble keeping his eyes down. Ibn Fahad and I agreed between ourselves to maintain that Mohammad had fallen prey to a wolf or some other beast, but our fellow travelers found it hard even to pretend belief. Only the Under-Vizier and the clerk Abdallah seemed to have their wits fully about them, and Abdallah made no secret of his contempt for the others. We set out again at once.

Our company was somber that day—and no wonder. No one wished to speak of the obvious, nor did they have much stomach for talk of lighter things. It was a silent file of people that moved through the mountain fastnesses.

As the shadows of evening began to roll down, the dark shape was with us again, flitting along just in sight, disappearing for a while only to return, bobbing along behind us like a jackdaw.

44

My skin was crawling—as you may well believe—though I tried to hide it.

We set camp, building a large fire and moving near to it, and had a sullen, close-cramped supper. Our supplies had dwindled so low that there was only a little desert bread and thin soup for each of us, and that hardly spiced at all. As has been written, an empty stomach makes a poor companion, always grumbling.

Ibrahim glared at the local plants, saying he wished he had more lore, as he was sure some of them must be edible. The peasant-boy claimed to know nothing about such things, and when the girl pointed and spoke about one or two of the plants, the boy refused to translate. Both Armenite youngsters quieted completely with the onset of darkness, drawing together as though they had called a truce.

Ibn Fahad, Abdallah, the Under-Vizier, and I were still speaking of the follower only as some beast. Abdallah may even have believed it—not from ordinary foolishness, but because he was the type of man who was unwilling to believe there might be anything he himself could not encompass.

As we took turns standing guard the young mullah led the far-from-sleepy men in prayer. The voices rose up with the smoke, neither seeming to be of much substance against the wind of those old, cold mountains.

I sidled over to the peasant-lad. He'd become, if anything, more close-mouthed since the discovery of the morning. The girl stayed close beside him, leaning against his shoulder, her eyes on me, wide and alert. Her mouth was set in a straight line.

"This 'vampyr' you spoke of . . ." I said quietly. "What do your people do to protect themselves from it?"

He looked up at me with a sad smile.

"We bar the doors."

I stared across at the other men—young Fawn with clenched mouth and furrowed brow; the mullah Ruad, eyes closed, plump cheeks awash with sweat as he prayed; the Under-Vizier turning his jewel-handled knife over and over in his hands, staring at it as though he did not see it or know its purpose; Ibrahim oiling a whetstone and sharpening his curved blade, glancing up now and then toward the darkness; Ibn Fahad gazing coolly outward, ever outward—and then I returned the boy's sad smile.

"No doors to lock, no windows to bar," I said. "What else?"

He consulted briefly with Sossi, who shook her head. "There is an herb we hang about our houses . . ." he said, and fumbled for the word in our unfamiliar language. After a moment he gave up. "It does not matter. We have none. None grows here."

I leaned forward, putting my face next to his face. "For the love of God, boy, what else?" —I knew it was not a beast of the earth. I *knew*. I too had seen that fluttering shadow.

He stared a moment at me. Sossi murmured something to him. "Well . . ." he mumbled, turning his face away, ". . . they say, some do, that you can tell stories . . ."

"What!" I thought he had gone mad.

"This is what my grandfather says. The vampyr will stop to hear the story you tell—if it is a good one—and if you continue it until daylight he must return to the . . . place of the dead."

There was a sudden shriek. I leaped to my feet, fumbling for my knife . . . but it was only Ruad, who had put his foot against a hot coal. I sank down again, heart hammering.

"Stories?" I asked.

"I have only heard so," he said, struggling for the right phrases. "We try to keep them farther away than that—they must come close to hear a man talking."

Later, after the fire had gone down, we placed sentries—from now on they would be in pairs—and went to our blankets. I lay a long while thinking of what the Armenite boy had said before I slept.

Chapter 6:

ATTACKED

A hideous screeching sound woke me. It was not yet dawn, and this time no one had burned himself on a glowing ember.

Bekir, one of the two soldiers who had been standing picket, lay on the forest floor within a few paces of the fire and the rest of our party, blood gouting from a great wound on the side of his head; in the torchlight it looked as though his skull had been smashed with a heavy cudgel. His drawn sword lay a short distance from him, the tip of the blade broken off. Achmed, the other sentry, was gone, but I heard a terrible thrashing in the underbrush beyond the camp, and screams that would have sounded like an animal in a cruel trap but for the half-formed words that bubbled up from time to time.

We crouched, huddled, staring like startled rabbits at the surrounding darkness. The screaming began to die away. Suddenly Ruad started up, heavy and clumsy getting to his feet. I saw tears in his eyes. "We . . . we must not leave our fellow to s-s-suffer so!" he cried, and looked around at all of us. I don't think anyone could hold his eye except the clerk Abdallah. I could not.

"Be silent, fool!" the clerk said, heedless of blaspheming a holy man. "It is a wild beast. It is for these cowardly soldiers to attend to, not a priest of God!"

The young mullah stared at him for a moment, and a change came over his face. The tears were still wet on his cheeks, but I saw his jaw firm and his shoulders square.

"No," he said. "We cannot leave him to Shaitan's servant. If you will not go to him, I will." He rolled up the scroll he had been nervously fingering and kissed it. A shaft of moonlight played across the gold letters.

I tried to grab his arm as he went past me, but he shook me off with surprising strength, then moved toward the brush, where the screeching had died down to a low, broken moaning.

"Come back, you idiot!" Abdallah shrieked at him. "This is foolishness! Come back!"

The young holy man looked back over his

shoulder, darting a look at Abdallah that I could not easily describe, then turned around and continued forward, holding the parchment scroll before him as if it were a candle against the dark night.

Ibn Fahad rose to his feet, his hand on the hilt of his sword. A moment he stood, staring at Ruad's back. He took two steps, then glanced at me. I could not meet his eyes—the sentry's broken blade, the night attack, the awful bubbling noises in the distance had all taken a toll on my courage. Ibn Fahad was too wise to follow the mullah alone, yet restlessness possessed him. He stood, one hand on his sword, listening to the night like the rest of us.

"There is no God but Allah!" I heard Ruad cry as he pushed into the underbrush, *"and Mohammad is His prophet!"* Then he was gone.

After a long moment there came the sound of the holy words of the Koran, chanted in an unsteady voice. We could hear the mullah making his ungraceful way through the thicket. I was not the only one who held his breath.

Next there was crashing, and branches snapping, as though some huge beast was leaping through the brush; the mullah's chanting became a howl. Men cursed helplessly. Before the cry had faded, though, another scream came—numbingly loud, the rage of a powerful animal, full of shock and surprise. It had words in it, although not in

any tongue I had ever heard before, or have heard since.

Another great thrashing, and then nothing but silence. We lit another fire and sat sleepless until dawn.

Chapter 7:

AN ARMOR OF TALES

In the morning, despite my urgings, the company went to look for any trace of the sentry and the young priest. They found them both.

It made a grim picture, my friends, let me tell you. They both hung upside down from the branches of a great tree. Their necks were torn, and they were white as chalk: All the blood had been drawn from them. The Armenite boy and girl stared at this spectacle, then both made a gesture over their faces and chests. They murmured unintelligible words; if it was prayer they uttered, they were not alone. There was nothing clean about this death.

We dragged the two stone-cold husks back to

the camp-circle, and shortly thereafter buried them commonly with the other sentry, who had not survived his head wound.

One curious thing there was: On the ground beneath the hanging head of the young priest lay the remains of his holy scroll. It was scorched to black ash, and crumbled at my touch.

"So it *was* a cry of pain we heard," said Ibn Fahad over my shoulder. "The devil-beast can be hurt, it appears."

"Hurt, but not made to give over," I observed. "And no other holy writings remain, nor any hands so holy to wield them or mouth to speak them." I looked pointedly over at Abdallah, who was giving unwanted instructions to Nizam and Ibrahim on how to spade the funeral dirt. I half-hoped one of them would take it on himself to brain the old meddler.

"True," grunted Ibn Fahad. "Well, I have my doubts on how cold steel will fare, also."

I remembered Bekir's broken blade. "As do I. But it could be there is yet a way we may save ourselves. The Armenite boy told me of it. I will explain when we stop at midday."

"I will be waiting eagerly," said Ibn Fahad, favoring me with his half-smile. "I am glad to see someone else is thinking and planning besides myself. But perhaps you should tell us your plan on the march. Our daylight hours are becoming precious as blood, now. As a matter of fact, I think from now on we shall have to do without lengthy burial services."

Well, there we were in a very nasty predicament. As we walked I explained my plan to the group; they listened silently, downcast, like people condemned to death—not an unreasonable attitude, in all truth.

"Now, here's the thing," I told them. "If this young lout's idea of tale-telling will work, we shall have to spend our nights yarning away. We may have to begin taking stops for sleeping in the daylight. Every moment walking, then, is precious—we must keep the pace up or we will die in these damned, haunted mountains. Also, while you walk, think of stories. From what the lad says we may have another fortnight or more to go until we escape this country. We shall soon run out of things to tell about unless you dig deep into your memories."

There was grumbling, but it was too dispirited a group to offer much protest.

"Be silent, unless you have a better idea," said Ibn Fahad. "Masrur is quite correct—although, if what I suspect is true, it may be the first time in his life he finds himself in that position." He threw me a wicked grin, and one of the soldiers snickered. It was a good sound to hear.

We had a short midday rest—most of us got at least an hour's sleep on the rocky ground—and then we walked on until the beginning of twilight. We were in the bottom of a long, thickly forested ravine, where we promptly built a large fire to keep away some of the darkness of the valley floor. Ah, but fire is a good friend!

Before full darkness fell, we all, including the girl, scavenged for wood. Tonight we would not let the fire burn down to embers. Even though its glow had not saved our sentries the night before, it gave us a sense of security: One cannot fight what one cannot see.

Ibn Fahad brought down another deer, a young doe. When he carried it back into camp and dumped it on the ground before Ibrahim, we all felt our spirits rise a little. Hard times are always easier to bear when your belly's full.

Gathered around the blaze, we cooked strips of venison on the ends of green sticks. Ibrahim doled out precious salt to us. We passed the water skin and wished it was more than water—not for the first time.

"Now then," I said, "I'll go first, for at home I was the one called upon most often to tell tales, and I have a good fund of them. Some of you may sleep, but not all—there should always be two or three awake in case the teller falters or forgets. We cannot know if this will keep the creature at bay, but we should take no chances."

So I began, telling first the story of the Four Clever Brothers. It was early, and no one was ready to sleep; all listened attentively as I spun it out, adding details here, stretching a description there. When I reached the place where the four brothers were being entertained by the Jinn's wife in the magic cavern before her husband returned, I dwelt long and lovingly upon the savor of the spices, cardamom, saffron, anise, cinnamon, clove, the black and red pepper, the delights of clarified ghee butter and goat meat, the lavish tastes of the sweetmeats, the celestial fragrances of incense, the bitterness of the strong coffee following the meal—all the blessings of civilization— until Ibn Fahad poked my thigh and muttered, "You are not helping morale."

(By the way, I would like to dispute that point, Ibn Fahad, old friend, even so long after the event. You see, I dwelt so lovingly on those details with two purposes in mind. The first was, of course, to stretch the tale out to its utmost limit, since I knew then that we might run short of things to tell before long. But there was another reason as well. Men whose minds were fixed on the things their tongues could not taste nor their noses savor were not thinking so much of the horror that awaited us in the forest: A fine tale can carry one away from discomfort. See, even as now, while you listen to me, you have forgotten your own small discomforts, have you not? But

Allah, my throat is dry from this thirsty work of tale-telling! Why has not Baba returned with the wine? Have you set a guard on your cellar, Abu Jamir? I warn you, this will not suffice to deter Baba. Many a time I have set him an impossible task, and though he might not accomplish it immediately, at length he has completed it. But I have lost my thread . . . Ah, morale. Yes, Ibn Fahad, although I did not agree, at your urging I ceased to detail the various delights the Four Brothers sampled and continued on to the end of the tale.)

When it ended I was applauded, and straight away began telling the story of the carpet merchant Salim and his unfaithful wife. That was perhaps not a good choice—it is a story about a vengeful jinn and about death; but I went on nonetheless, finished it, then told two more.

As I was ending the fourth story, about a brave orphan who finds a cave of jewels and outwits forty thieves, I glimpsed a strange thing.

The fire had died down a bit, and as I looked out over the flames I saw movement in the forest. The Under-Vizier Walid was directly across from me, and beyond his once-splendid robes a dark shape lurked. It came no closer than the edge of the trees, staying just out of the fire's flickering light. I lost my voice for a moment, then stuttered, but quickly caught up the thread of the story and finished. No one had noticed, I was sure.

I asked for the waterskin and motioned for Walid al-Salameh to continue. He took up with a tale of the rivalry between two wealthy houses in his native Isfahan. One or two of the others wrapped themselves tightly in their cloaks and lay down, staring up as they listened, watching the sparks rise into the darkness.

I pulled my hood down low on my brow to shield my gaze, then squinted out past Walid's shoulder. The dark shape had moved a little nearer now to the lapping glow of the campfire.

It was man-shaped, that I could see fairly well, though it clung close to the trunk of a tree at clearing's edge. Its face was in darkness. Two ember-red eyes unblinkingly reflected the firelight. It seemed clothed in rags, but that could have been a trick of the shadows.

Huddled in the darkness a stone's throw away, it was listening.

I turned my head slowly across the circle. Most eyes were on the Under-Vizier, even those of Kurken and Sossi, who could not have understood much of what he said; Fawn had curtained his in sleep, and Abdallah watched the young man, seeming not to listen to Walid's words. But Ibn Fahad was staring out into the darkness. I suppose he felt my gaze, for he turned to me and nodded slightly: he had seen it too.

We went on until dawn, the men taking turns sleeping as one of the others told stories—mostly tales they had heard as children, occasionally of an adventure that had befallen them. Ibn Fahad and I said nothing of the dark shape that watched. Somewhere in the hour before dawn it disappeared.

It was a sleepy group that took to the trail that day, but we had all lived through the night. This alone put the men in better spirits, and we covered much ground.

The following evening we again sat around the fire. I told the story of the Gazelle King, and then the story of the Enchanted Peacock, followed by the story of the Little Man with No Name, each tale longer and more complicated than the one before. Everyone except the clerk Abdallah contributed something—Abdallah and the Armenite boy and girl, that is. The chief-clerk said repeatedly that he had never wasted his time on foolishness such as learning stories. We did not force him, reluctant—as you might guess—to press our self-preservation into such unwilling hands.

The Armenite boy, our guide, sat quietly all the evening and listened to the men yarning away in a tongue that was not his own, but one that he was mastering day by day, for he and the Under-

Vizier still spoke as we marched. Sossi, who had begun aiding Ibrahim with cooking and other tasks, was also learning a few of our words. She huddled against Kurken, and occasionally they whispered to each other. At length the girl fell into sleep, but her lover remained awake, listening with the rest of us. When the moon had risen through the treetops, the shadow returned and stood silently outside the clearing. I saw the peasant lad look up. He saw it, I know, but like Ibn Fahad and me, he held his tongue.

The next day brought us disaster.

Chapter 8:
DEATH OUR COMPANION

As we were striking camp in the morning, happily no fewer than when we had sat down the night before, Ibrahim and Kurken took our waterskins down to a stream, a journey involving climbing down rocks on a small cliff face. I had done the same duty the night before with Nizam, the younger of the pikemen, and I did not envy them their chore. The climb back up with full waterskins was especially grueling.

They had not been gone long enough for us to stow all our gear when we heard a cry, and then a horrid thud. Ibn Fahad and I raced to the clifftop and looked over.

Ibrahim lay at the base of the cliff, the Armenite boy kneeling beside him. One of the waterskins had burst, splashing the rocks around the Turk. For a moment I had the unpleasant thought that the boy had engineered this accident, though I could think of no reason why he should do so in the face of our troubles. I gave a cry. The boy looked up.

"He fell," Ibn Fahad said, "and struck his head on a rock. He still breathes."

Ibn Fahad ran back to camp and returned with a rope; then I made the perilous descent down the cliff face for the second time in two days. The Under-Vizier, the two remaining soldiers Nizam and Hamed, and Fawn had accompanied Ibn Fahad from camp; they all stood at the top of the cliff, ready to aid. The Armenite boy and I crafted a harness from one end of the rope and fastened it around Ibrahim's torso. The men at top pulled and we climbed up behind, guiding, until we got the Turk to the top of the cliff and thence into camp.

Ibn Fahad suggested that someone must fetch up our other three waterskins, for we needed them now more than ever. I made the hellish descent a third time, not without making my displeasure known. This time, the boy stood at the top of the cliff, tossed the rope down, and I tied the waterskins on. With his pulling and my guiding, we accomplished the task much more easily. I cursed myself that we had not thought of this method earlier.

When we arrived back at camp, the Armenite

girl was kneeling beside the Turk, touching his throat to feel for his pulse. She said something to Kurken, who came forward with his waterskin and spilled some of the water over a kerchief she produced from a pocket. She bathed the Turk's face with water, then glanced up at us, the circle of men looking down at her. I too glanced around at us. The Under-Vizier looked concerned and uneasy. Fawn looked stricken. Ibn Fahad held his own counsel; even his mustache-ends were still. Nizam and Hamed had foreheads furrowed with worry. The Armenite boy bit his bottom lip. And Abdallah! Abdallah wore a sour mouth and a pinched nose, as if he had smelled offal.

"Perhaps if we leave him here, the creature will feast on him tonight, and leave the rest of us free to journey on," he said.

"Shut your mouth," I growled. I felt a sickness touch my stomach. As terrible as his suggestion was, what sickened me even more was the fact that I had considered it too for an instant.

The girl spoke. The Under-Vizier translated: "Does anyone here know anything of medicine?"

Thankful for any distraction to lead us away from the unthinkable, all spoke out loudly and immediately to confess that we did not.

"Am I a Christian, or a Jew?" asked Hamed, affronted.

"I know a bit of rough soldier's doctoring," Ibn Fahad said. "Enough to bandage a wound.

Where did he strike the rock?" He knelt beside the Turk and gently lifted his head, feeling beneath Ibrahim's turban. "By Allah, there is a lump here big as a chicken's egg!" He grasped the girl's hand and directed it to the right side of the Turk's head. She gasped as she touched the swelling. Then she spoke again.

"She knows a few simple remedies," Walid translated. "She can make a poultice for this, and there is a plant which grows here that will awaken sleepers."

The girl rose and went to the forest's edge and vanished beneath the trees. By the time she returned with bits of greenery clutched in her hands, Ibrahim was showing signs of life, his body twitching, his head rolling a little. Ibn Fahad had taken a strip off his sash and a piece of the hem from his *aba* and rinsed them both. Fawn was still bathing the slave's forehead with cool water and the girl's kerchief.

"Pardon," she said, the first Arabic word I had heard from her lips. She gently pushed Fawn aside. She took the strips of cloth Ibn Fahad proffered, wrapped some of her plants in the piece of hem, crushed it between two stones, soaked it in water, and bound it against Ibrahim's head over the swelling, using the strip of Ibn Fahad's sash to fasten it in place. The other plant she crushed and held below Ibrahim's nose. Its pungent odor rose on the damp morning air and made me sneeze. I was not alone in my response; Ibrahim sneezed also, and struggled to rise before weakness overcame him and he fell back. Only one of his arms aided him; his left arm hung limply.

"Uncle?" murmured the Armenite girl, dropping her herb and catching Ibrahim's right hand. "Uncle?"

The slave closed his eyes and lay silent for a long moment. His hand tightened on the girl's. Groaning, he made another attempt to rise, but his left arm lay as if dead. When his eyes opened again, they were wet and frightened.

Later that day, in the early afternoon, the second blow fell.

Ibrahim had lost the use of his left arm, and his left leg obeyed his commands only stiffly. Fawn cut a stick for him and stripped it of twigs. Grasping the stick in his right hand, Ibrahim used it as a third leg, to steady him on the slippery wet clay. Sossi stood at his left side, clutching his dead arm around her shoulders, supporting him. For the first time it came to me to bless Allah that Ibrahim was a small cricket of a man, weighing little; it was not such a hardship to help him over the rough places as it would have been with myself or one of the other soldiers. Still, although we took it in turns to aid him, our progress slowed measurably.

We were coming up out of the valley, climbing diagonally along the steep side of the ravine. The damned Caucassian fogs had slimed the rocks and turned the ground soggy so that the footing was treacherous.

Hamed, the older of the remaining pike-men, had been walking poorly all day. He had bad joints, and the cold nights out-of-doors had been making them worse.

We had stopped to rest on an outcropping of rock that jutted from the valley wall; and Hamed, the last in line, was just catching up to us when he slipped. He fell heavily onto his side and slid several feet down the muddy slope.

Ibn Fahad jumped up to look for a rope, but before he could get one from the bottom of his pack, the other soldier, Nizam, clambered down the grade to help his comrade.

He got a grip on Hamed's tunic, and was just turning around to catch Ibn Fahad's rope when the leg of the older man buckled beneath him and he fell backward. Nizam, caught off his balance, pitched back as well, his hand caught in the neck of Hamed's garment, and the two of them rolled end over end down the slope. Before anyone could so much as cry out they had both disappeared over the edge, like a wine jug rolling off a table-top.

To fall such a distance certainly killed them.

We could not find the bodies, of course . . . could not even climb back down the ravine to look. Ibn Fahad's remark about burials had taken on a terrible, ironic truth. We could but press on now, a party of eight—myself, Ibn Fahad, the Under-Vizier Walid, Abdallah the clerk, Ibrahim the slave, the two Armenite youngsters, and young Fawn. I doubt that there was a single one of our number who did not wonder which of us would next meet death in that lonesome place.

Chapter 9:
AN INVITATION

Ah, by Allah most high, I have never been so sick of the sound of my own voice as I was by the time nine more nights had passed. Ibn Fahad, I know, would say that I have never understood how sick *everyone* becomes of the sound of my voice—am I correct, old friend? But I *was* tired of it, tired of talking all night, tired of racking my brain for stories, tired of listening to the cracked voices of Walid and Ibn Fahad and Fawn; of the voice of Ibrahim, speaking with the new pain of feeling useless, he who had delighted in his work and now could no longer accomplish it. The only novelty, and it was a small one, was the rare times when Sossi would speak, her voice soft, and Kurken would translate what she said into stumbling Arabic. (Though he was learning our tongue, aided by Walid and long nights of listening, he seemed to have no imagination for tales himself.) Soon, though, even the strangeness of foreign tales palled. And I was tired to sickness of the damp, gray, oppressive mountains, whose skies granted us little light by day and only terror by night. But, of course, I would have gladly suffered a year of such monotony in trade for passage out of those mountains and out of the reach of the thing that stalked us. The question was how long we could go on before our failing voices and fading courage gave out, or before our supply of tales, now virtually empty, was drained to the bottom of the jar.

We stumbled through the days like sleepwalkers, locked into nightmares, so that it was a wonder that no more of us emulated our two hapless pikemen by tumbling into ravines, or down slopes. I know I was too weary to watch my own footing, and in these latter days I can only believe Allah preserved me across those desolate pathways for some other purpose—though Ibn Fahad would say it puzzles the sages what that purpose might be.

All were now aware of the haunting shade that stood outside our fire at night, waiting and listening. Young Fawn, in particular, could hardly hold up his turn at tale-telling, so much did his voice tremble. Even when he told humorous tales, somehow corpses appeared in them, until one of us would call a halt and take over the tales, trying to drive them onto friendlier ground.

Abdallah grew steadily colder and colder, congealing like rendered fat. The thing which followed us, hunted us, was no respecter of his cynicism or of his mathematics, and would not be banished for all the scorn he could muster. The skinny chief-clerk did not try to support the story circle with us, but sat silently and walked apart. Despite our terrible mutual danger he avoided our company as much as possible, though I noticed that when Fawn took up the thread of a tale, Abdallah would wake and watch him. But the clerk did few of the tasks incumbent upon all of us to survive, disdaining even to take a turn at aiding Ibrahim.

The tenth night after the loss of Nizam and Hamed, we were running out of tales. We had been ground down by our circumstances, and were ourselves becoming nearly as shadowy as that which we feared.

In the second quarter of the night, during the darkest hours, Walid al-Salameh was droning on about some ancient bit of minor intrigue from the court of the Emperor Darius of Persia. Ibn Fahad leaned toward me, lowering his voice so that none of the others could hear.

"Did you notice," he whispered, "that our guest has made no appearance tonight?"

"It has not escaped me," I said. "I hardly think it is a good sign, however. If our talk no longer interests the creature, how long can it be until its thoughts return to our other uses?" I glanced at the Armenite boy and girl, huddled in each other's arms, both with faces slack in sleep, and at Ibrahim, twisted awkwardly, his left arm tied up in a sling made of someone's spare turban, but withal leaning forward as if hanging upon the Under-Vizier's words.

"I fear you're right," he responded, and gave a scratchy, painful chuckle. "There's a good three or four more days' walking—and hard walking at that, if no other unforeseen gift of Fate descends upon us—until we reach the bottom of these mountains and come once more onto the plain, at which point we might hope the devil-beast would leave us."

"Ibn Fahad," I said, shaking my head as I looked across at Fawn's drawn, pale face, "I fear we shall not manage . . ." As if to point up the truth of my fears, Walid here stopped his speech, coughing violently. I gave him to drink of the waterskin, but when he had swallowed he did not begin anew; he only sat looking darkly, as one lost, out to the forest.

"Good Vizier," I asked, "can you continue?"

He said nothing, and I quickly spoke in his place, trying to pick up the threads of a tale I had not been attending to. Walid leaned back, exhausted and breathing raggedly. Abdallah clucked his tongue in disgust. If I had not been fearfully occupied, I would have struck the clerk.

71

Just as I was beginning to find my way, inventing a continuation of the vizier's Darian political meanderings, there came a shock that passed through all of us like a cold wind. A new shadow appeared at the edge of the clearing.

The vampyr had rejoined us.

Walid moaned and sat up, huddling by the fire. I faltered for a moment but went on. The candle-flame eyes regarded us unblinkingly, and the shadow shook for a moment as if folding great wings.

Suddenly Fawn leaped to his feet, swaying unsteadily. I lost the strands of the story completely and stared up at him in amazement.

"*Creature!*" he screamed. "*Hell-spawn!* Why do you torment us in this way? Why, why, why?"

Ibn Fahad reached up to pull him down, but the young man danced away like a shying horse. His mouth hung open and his eyes were starting from their dark-rimmed sockets.

"You great beast!" he continued to shriek. "Why do you toy with us? Why do you not just kill me—kill us *all*, set us free from this terrible, terrible . . ."

And with that he walked *forward*—away from the fire, toward the thing that crouched at the forest's edge.

Chapter 10:
A NEW VOICE

"End this now!" Fawn shouted, and fell to his knees only a few strides from the smoldering red eyes, sobbing like a child.

"Stupid boy, get back!" I cried. Before I could get up to pull him back—and I would have, I swear by Allah's name—there was a great rushing noise, and the black shape was gone, the lamps of its stare extinguished. Then, as we pulled the helplessly shuddering youth back to the campfire, something rustled in the trees. On the opposite side of the campfire one of the near branches suddenly bobbed beneath the weight of a strange new fruit—a great black thing with red-lit eyes. It made an awful croaking noise.

In our shock it was a few moments before we

realized that the deep, rasping sound was speech—
and the words were Arabic!

"It . . . was . . . you . . ." it said, ". . . *who
chose . . . to play the game this way. . . .*"

Almost strangest of all, I would swear that
this thing had never spoken our language before,
never even heard it until we had wandered lost
into the mountains. Something of its halting in-
flections, its strange hesitations, made me guess it
had learned our speech from listening all these
nights to our campfire stories.

"Demon!" shrilled Abdallah. "What manner
of creature are you?!"

"You know . . . very well what kind of . . .
thing I am, man. None of you may know *how*, or
why . . . but by now you know *what* I am."

"Why? Why do you torment us so?!" shouted
Fawn, writhing in Ibn Fahad's strong grasp.

"Why does the . . . serpent kill . . . a rabbit?
The serpent does not . . . hate. It kills to live, as
do I . . . as do you."

Abdallah lurched forward a step. "We do not
slaughter our fellow men like this, devil-spawn!"

"C-c-clerk!" the black shape growled, and
dropped down from the tree. "C-close your fool-
ish mouth! You push me too far!" It bobbed, as
if agitated. "The curse of human ways! Even now
you provoke me more than you should, you
huffing . . . insect! *Enough!*"

The vampyr hesitated, then sprang upward

once more, into the shadowy trees. With a great rattling of leaves he scuttled away along a limb. I was fumbling for my sword, but before I could find it the creature spoke again from his high perch.

"The young one asked me why I 'toy' with you. I do not. If I do not kill, I will suffer. More than I suffer already.

"Despite what this clerk says, though, I am not a creature without . . . without feelings as men have them. Less and less do I wish to destroy you.

"For the first time in a great age I have listened to the sound of human voices that were not screaming in fear. I have approached a circle of humans without the barking of dogs, and have listened to them talk.

"It has almost been like being a man again."

"And this is how you show your pleasure?" the Under-Vizier Walid asked, teeth chattering. "By k-k-killing us?"

"I am what I am," said the beast. "But for all that, you have inspired a certain desire for companionship. It puts me in mind of things that I can barely remember.

"I propose we make a . . . bargain," said the vampyr. "A . . . *wager?*"

I had found my sword, and Ibn Fahad had drawn his as well, but we both knew we could not kill a thing like this—a red-eyed demon that could leap five cubits in the air and had learned to speak our language in a fortnight. If this was one of the People of the Fire, such as the Jinni and the Ifrits, it was far beyond any means within our power to end its existence.

"No bargains with Shaitan!" spat the clerk Abdallah.

"What do you mean, creature?" I demanded, inwardly marveling that such an unlikely dialogue should ever take place on the earth. "Pay no attention to the"—I curled my lip—"holy man." Abdallah shot me a venomous glance.

"Hear me, then," the creature said, and in the deep recesses of the tree seemed once more to unfold and stretch great wings. "Hear me. I must kill to live, and my nature is such that I cannot choose to die. That is the way of things.

"I offer you now, however, the chance to win safe passage out of my domain, these hills. We shall have a contest, a wager if you like; if you best me you shall go freely, and I shall turn once more to the musty, slow-blooded peasants of the local valleys."

Sossi's eyes burned and her nostrils flared at that, as though she understood what the thing said. The vampyr had not been the only creature to learn something from our night tales.

Ibn Fahad laughed bitterly. "What, are we to fight you then? So be it!"

"I would snap your spine like a dry branch," croaked the black shape. "No, you have held me these many nights telling stories; it is story-telling that will win you safe passage. We will have a contest, one that will suit my whims: We shall strive to tell the saddest of all stories. Do you understand? The saddest. That is my demand. You may each tell one, and I also will tell one. If you can best me with any or all, you shall go unhindered by me."

"And if we lose?" I cried. "And, in any case, who shall judge?"

"*You* may judge," it said, and the deep, thick voice took on a tone of grim amusement. "If you can look into my eyes and tell me that you have bested *my* sad tale . . . why, then I shall believe you.

"If you lose," it continued, "then one of your number shall be given to me to pay the price of your defeat . . . and I will consume that prize while you watch. Those are my terms; otherwise I shall hunt you down one at a time—for in truth, your present tale-telling has begun to lose my interest."

Ibn Fahad darted a worried look in my direction. Fawn and the others stared at the demon-shape in mute terror and astonishment.

"We shall . . . we shall give you our decision at sunset tomorrow," I said. "We must be allowed to think and talk."

"As you wish," said the vampyr. "But if you accept my challenge, the game must begin then.

After all, we have only a few more days to spend together." And at this the terrible creature laughed, a sound like the bark being pulled from the trunk of a rotted tree. Then the shadow was gone.

Chapter 11:

WAGERING OUR LIVES

In the end we had to accede to the creature's wager, of course. It was our only chance. We knew he was not wrong in his assessment of us— we were just wagging our beards over the nightly campfire, no longer even listening to our own tales. Whatever magic had held the vampyr at bay had long since drained from us like meal from a torn sack.

As we walked, making as much distance as we could on what would possibly be the last day for one or more of us, I racked my poor brains for stories of sadness, but could think of nothing that seemed to fit, nothing that seemed significant enough for the vital purpose at hand. I had been doing most of the talking for several nights running, and had exhausted virtually every story I had ever heard—and I was never much good at making them up, as Ibn Fahad will attest. (Yes, go ahead and smile, old comrade.)

Then I bethought me of a dark-eyed woman I had glimpsed but once, and the sadness I felt at the thought that I might never again glimpse such a one, never smell the sweet richness of her perfumes of aloewood and ambergris and musk, or spy a petaled flower hennaed on her palm, this sadness was so strong and swift in me that I knew a story would come to me, though I did not at that time know what it might be.

Actually, it was Ibn Fahad who volunteered the first tale. I asked him what it was, but he would not tell me. "Let me save what potency it may have," he said.

The Under-Vizier Walid also had something he deemed suitable.

Kurken and Sossi spoke to each other in their hard-edged tongue, glancing at the rest of us as they did. I saw in their glances a resentment I had thought the terrible journey to have crushed by now. At last Kurken said, "We too have a tale—one between us."

"My injury has given me a new way of looking at things," said Ibrahim slowly, as if speaking had become as laborious as walking. "I remember now the tale I wish to tell, though I did not like it nor understand it when I first heard it."

I was still racking my brain when young Fawn piped up that he had thought of his tale as well. I looked him over, rosy cheeks and long-lashed eyes, and asked him what he could possibly know of sadness. Even as I spoke I realized my cruelty, standing as we all did in the shadow of death or worse, but it was too late to take it back.

Fawn did not flinch. He was folding his cloak as he sat cross-ankled on the ground, folding and unfolding it. He looked up and said: "I shall tell a sad story about love. All the saddest stories are about love."

Abdallah continued to offer nothing but his cynical sneer. The idea that, if our luck failed, his sour face might be the last thing I saw was sadder than almost any tale I have *ever* heard of, but I decided it would not much impress our enemy.

We walked as fast and far as we could that day, as if hoping that somehow, against all reason, we should find ourselves out of the gloomy, mist-sodden hills. But when twilight came the vast bulk of the mountains still hung above us. We made camp on the porch of a great standing rock, as though protection at our backs would avail us something if the night went badly.

The fire had only just taken hold—the sun had dipped below the rim of the hills but a moment before—when a cold wind made the branches of the trees whip back and forth. We knew without speaking, without looking at one another, that the creature had come.

"Have you made your decision?" The harsh voice from the trees sounded strange, as if its owner was trying to speak lightly, carelessly—but I heard only death in those cold syllables.

"We have," said Ibn Fahad, drawing himself up out of his involuntary half-crouch to stand erect. "We will accept your wager. Do you wish to begin?"

"Oh, no . . ." the thing said, and made a flapping noise. "That would take all of the . . . suspense from the contest, would it not? No, I insist that you begin."

"I am first, then," Ibn Fahad said, looking around our circle for confirmation. The dark shape moved abruptly toward us. Before we could scatter the vampyr stopped, a few short steps away.

"Do not fear," it grated. Close to one's ear the voice was even odder and more strained. "I have come nearer to hear the story and see the teller—for surely that is part of any tale—but I shall move no farther. Begin."

Everybody but myself stared into the fire, hugging their knees, keeping their eyes averted from the bundle of darkness that sat at our shoulders. I had the fire between myself and the creature, and felt safer than if I had sat like Walid and Ibrahim and Abdallah, with nothing between the beast and my back but cold ground.

The vampyr sat hunched, as if imitating our posture, its eyes hooded so that only a flicker of scarlet light, like a half-buried brand, showed through the slit. It was black, this manlike thing— not black like an African tribesman, mind you, but black as burnt steel, black as the mouth of a cave. It bore the aspect of someone dead of the plague. Rags wrapped it, mouldering, filthy bits of cloth, rotten as old bread . . . but the curve of its back spoke of terrible life—a great black cricket poised to jump.

Chapter 12:

THE TALE OF IBN FAHAD

Many years ago [Ibn Fahad began] I traveled for
a good while in Egypt. I was indigent, then, and
journeyed wherever the prospect of payment for a
sword arm beckoned.

I found myself at last in the household guard
of a rich merchant in Alexandria. I was happy
enough there, and I enjoyed walking in the busy
streets, their bustle so unlike the village in which
I was born.

One summer evening I found myself on an
unfamiliar street. It emptied out into a little square
that sat below the front of an old mosque. The
square was full of people, merchants and fish-
wives, a juggler or two, but most of the crowd
was drawn up to the facade of the mosque, pressed
in close together.

At first, as I strolled across the square, I thought prayers were about to begin, but it was still some time until sunset. I wondered if perhaps some notable *imam* was speaking from the mosque steps, but as I approached I could see that all the assembly were staring upward, craning their necks back as if the sun itself, on its way to its western mooring, had become snagged on one of the minarets.

But instead of the sun, what stood on the onion-shaped dome was the silhouette of a man, who seemed to be staring out toward the horizon.

"Who is that?" I asked a man near me.

"It is Ha'arud al-Emwiya, the Sufi," the man told me, never lowering his eyes from the tower above.

"Is he caught up there?" I demanded. "Will he not fall?"

"Watch," was all the man said. I did.

A moment later, much to my horror, the small dark figure of Ha'arud the Sufi seemed to go rigid, then toppled from the minaret's rim like a stone. I gasped in shock, and so did a few others around me, but the rest of the crowd only stood in hushed attention.

Then an incredible thing happened. The tumbling holy man spread his arms out from his shoulders, like a bird's wings, and his downward fall became a swooping glide. He bottomed out high above the crowd, then sped upward, riding the wind like a leaf, spinning, somersaulting, stopping at last to drift to the ground as gently as a bit of down. Meanwhile, all the assembly was chanting "God is great! God is great!" When the Sufi had set down upon the earth with his bare feet the people surrounded him, touching his rough woolen garments and crying out his name. He said nothing, only stood and smiled, and before too long the people began to wander away, talking amongst themselves.

"But this is truly marvelous!" I said to the man who stood by me.

"Before every holy day he flies," the man said, then shrugged. "I am surprised this is the first time you have heard of Ha'arud al-Emwiya."

I was determined to speak to this amazing old man, and as the crowd dispersed I approached and asked if I might buy him a glass of tea. Close up he had a look of seamed roguishness that was surprising, placed against the great favor in which Allah must have held him. He smilingly agreed, and accompanied me to a tea shop close by in the Street of Weavers.

"How is it," I asked, "if you will pardon my forwardness, that you of all holy men are so gifted?"

He looked up from the tea cupped in his palms and grinned. He had only two teeth. "Balance," he said.

I was surprised. "A cat has balance," I re-

sponded, "but it nevertheless must wait for the pigeons to land before it catches them."

"I refer to a different sort of balance," he said. "The balance between Allah and Shaitan, which as you know, Allah the All-Knowing has created as an equilibrium of exquisite delicacy."

"Explain please, Master." I called for food, but Ha'arud refused any himself.

"In all things care must be exercised," he explained. "Thus it is too with my flying. Many men holier than I are as earthbound as stones. Many other men live so poorly as to shame the Devil himself, yet they cannot take to the air, either. Only I, if I may be excused what sounds self-satisfied, have discovered perfect balance. Thus, each year before the holy days I tote up my score carefully, committing small peccadilloes or acts of faith as needed until the weights are exactly, exactly balanced. Thus, when I jump from the mosque, neither Allah nor the Arch-Enemy has claim on my soul, and they bear me up until a later date, at which time the issue shall be clearer." He smiled again and drained his tea.

"You are . . . a sort of chessboard on which God and the Devil contend?" I asked, perplexed.

"A flying chessboard, yes," he laughed.

We talked for a long while, as the shadows grew long across the Street of the Weavers, but the Sufi Ha'arud adhered stubbornly to his explanation. I must have seemed disbelieving, for he finally proposed that we ascend to the top of the mosque so he could demonstrate.

I was more than a little drunk and he, imbibing only tea, was filled nonetheless with a strange gleefulness. We made our way up the many winding stairs and climbed out onto the narrow ledge that circled the minaret like a crown. The cool night air, and the thousands of winking lights of Alexandria far below, sobered me rapidly. "I suddenly find all your precepts very sound," I said. "Let us go down."

But Ha'arud would have none of it, and proceeded to step lightly off the edge of the dome. He hovered, like a bumblebee, a hundred feet above the dusty street. "Balance," he said with great satisfaction.

"But," I asked, "is the good deed of giving me this demonstration enough to offset the pride with which you exhibit your skill?" I was cold and wanted to get down; thus, I hoped to shorten the exhibition.

Instead, hearing my question, Ha'arud screwed up his face as though it was something he had not given thought to. A moment later, with a shriek of surprise, he plummeted down out of my sight to smash on the mosque's stone steps, as dead as dead.

Ibn Fahad, having lost himself in remembering the story, poked at the campfire. "Thus, the problem with matters of delicate balance," he said, and shook his head.

The whispering rustle of our dark visitor brought us sharply back. "Interesting," the creature rasped. "Sad, yes. Sad enough? We shall see. Who is the next of your number?"

A cold chill, like fever, swept over me at those calm words.

The Armenite girl Sossi, who had sat hidden within the folds of the black *taylasan* during Ibn Fahad's recital, at these words stirred, dropping the cloth from across her mouth. "We are prepared," she said in accented Arabic, then glanced at Kurken, who nodded.

Chapter 13:

THE TALE OF KURKEN AND SOSSI

First Sossi spoke, her voice light, but pronouncing most words in her own ugly language; afterward, Kurken translated, after consulting Walid about a few words such as "Caliph." As I listened, though, the doubled voices vanished beneath the weight of the tale.

Once there were two old married people with no children [the Armenites began]. The woman prayed to God, saying, "God, you give us food and shelter. You give us everything but a child. Please, God, give us a child. An earth-child, a rain-child, a fire-child, a shadow-child. We will love any child you give us."

God at last listened and gave the woman a shadow-child.

Each day the shadow-child grew a month big, and each month he grew a year big. But the shadow-child was only there in the day. At night when everything was shadows the shadow-child vanished, except near the *toneer*, the place of fire in the house, where light was. There you could see him, but if he walked away from the fire he vanished. His mother and father did not know if he was alive or dead in the dark.

The mother and father loved the shadow-child and called him a blessing from God. They taught him honor and tradition.

When the child was big enough to work in the harvest, he was so strong he could plow without oxen. He was strong, the shadow-child.

The father died, leaving the shadow-child to take care of his mother.

One day the shadow-child took the wool to market. On the way he saw an apricot tree behind a wall. A branch full of apricots orange as morning sun hung just on the other side. The shadow-child had to climb up and taste the apricots. When he was on the wall he saw the Caliph's daughter sitting by a fountain braiding her hair. She was so beautiful his heart filled with love. She looked up and saw him. She came to the wall. He gave her an apricot, then climbed down and ran away.

"Mother," he told the old woman when he came home, "I saw the one I will marry. Go to the palace and ask the Caliph for her hand."

"Very well, my son," she said, and went to the palace and asked the Caliph for his daughter's hand.

"Who are you, a woman in rags, to ask for my daughter for your son?" said the Caliph, and he had his servants beat her.

The shadow-child was sad when he saw his mother hurt. He did not ask her to go again to the palace but next day he sat and ate nothing. His mother did not want to see him sad so she went again to the Caliph's house.

The Caliph had his servants beat her harder the second time.

The shadow-child was even sadder when his mother came home. He did not like to see her hurt, but the Caliph's daughter was in his heart.

Still he would eat no food, so his mother went to the palace again. The Caliph was very angry, but saw that she would always come back even when she was beaten. He decided to give her son an impossible task and be rid of them both. He said, "If your son can bring me a jug of water from the stream that runs beside the sun's house, he can marry my daughter."

The mother told the shadow-child what the Caliph said.

The next day the shadow-child packed food and tied his mother's best water jug on his back. He walked toward the sunset where the sun's house was. He walked during the day and at night he vanished.

After walking forty days he found a deep hole in the ground at the end of the world. He lit a torch so he would not vanish and went down in the hole.

Very far under the ground he found a beautiful stream of water white as milk, shining like the moon. Near was a house built of white stone covered with gold letters. Behind the walls he saw the tops of trees. He smelled ripe fruit and heard birds singing. In the courtyard in front of the house sat the sun's mother, waiting for her child to come home.

The shadow-child waited for night. The water was so bright he thought it might keep him from vanishing even after sunset, and it would be easier to take the water after the sun went in to bed.

Soon the sun came down the tunnel and went to his mother, who hugged him and took him into the house. When the door closed the shadow-child filled his jug with water from the stream.

The water was bright like the sun, so as he climbed up the tunnel he did not vanish.

Behind him he heard the sun's mother cry: "Who took my water? Thief! In the morning my son will find you! He sees everything!"

The shadow-child traveled back home, hiding from the sun in the day, using the sun's water at night to light his way. He walked forty nights, hiding always from the sun who had been his friend. Then he came to his own house where his mother waited. She kissed him. Then together they went to the Caliph.

The Caliph could not break his promise. When the shadow-child gave him the jug of water from the sun's stream, he bowed his head.

The next day the shadow-child and the Caliph's daughter were married. The drinking and feasting lasted seven days and seven nights. On the last day, the Caliph brought the jug of the sun's water out to share with all at the feast. He told how the shadow-child had stolen the water.

High in the sky, the sun heard the whole story. At last he knew who was the thief.

"I will never again shine on the shadow-child," the sun said. So, in front of his new bride and his mother, the shadow-child vanished forever, leaving only darkness behind.

A moment's silence followed the Armenites' voices as they ceased their doubled tale. They looked at each other, their brows furrowed, as if there might be more to the tale; but where could it go? Kurken put his arm around Sossi's shoulder. Both of them stared at the vampyr.

His eyes burned very bright. For a moment

he said nothing. The hooding of wings he seemed to carry with him, though not distinct, rose above him, as if to shade him from the night sky.

"Sad," he said at last. "And I do not like this talk of the sun. Sad enough? We shall see. Who speaks next?"

". . . I am next . . ." said Fawn, voice taut as a bowstring. "Shall I begin?"

The vampyr said nothing, only bobbed the black lump of his head. The youth cleared his throat and began.

Chapter 14:
FAWN'S STORY

There was once . . . [Fawn began, and hesitated, then started again]. There was once a young prince named Zufik, the second son of a great sultan. Seeing no prospects for himself in his father's kingdom, he went out into the wild world to search for his fortune. He traveled through many lands, and saw many strange things, and heard tell of others stranger still.

In one place he was told of a nearby sultanate, the ruler of which had a beautiful daughter: His only child and the very apple of his eye.

Now this country had been plagued for several years by a terrible beast, a great white leopard of a kind never seen before. So fearsome it was that it had killed hunters sent to trap it, yet it was also so cunning that it had stolen babies from their very cradles as their mothers lay sleeping. The people of the sultanate all lived in fear; and the sultan, whose bravest, strongest warriors had tried and failed to kill the beast, was driven to despair. Finally, at the end of his wits, he had it proclaimed in the marketplace that the man who could destroy the white leopard would be gifted with the sultan's daughter Rassoril, and with her throne of the sultanate after the old man was gone.

Young Zufik heard how the best young men of the country, and others from countries beyond, had one after the other met their deaths beneath the claws of the leopard, or . . . or . . . in its jaws . . .

[Here I saw the boy Fawn hesitate, as if the vision of flashing teeth he was conjuring had suddenly reminded him of our predicament. Walid the Under-Vizier reached out and patted the lad's shoulder with great gentleness, until he was calm enough to resume.]

So . . . [He swallowed]. So young Prince Zufik took himself into that country, and soon he was announced at the sultan's court.

The ruler was a tired old man, the fires in his sunken eyes long quenched. Much of his power seemed to have been handed over to a pale, narrow-faced youth named Sifaz, who was the princess's cousin. As Zufik announced his purpose, as so many had done before him, Sifaz's eyes flashed.

"You will no doubt meet the end all the others have," the cousin said, "but you are welcome to the attempt—and the prize, should you win."

Then for the first time Zufik saw the princess Rassoril, and in an instant his heart was overthrown.

She had hair as black and shiny as polished jet, and a face upon which Allah himself must have looked in satisfaction, thinking: "Here is the summit of My art." Her delicate hands looked like tiny doves as they nested in her lap, and a man could fall into her brown eyes and drown without hope of rescue—which is what Zufik did, and he was not wrong when he thought he saw Rassoril return his ardent gaze.

Sifaz saw too, and his thin mouth turned into something like a smile. He narrowed his yellow eyes. "Take this princeling to his room, that he may sleep now and wake with the moon. The leopard's voice was heard around the palace's walls last night."

Indeed, when Zufik woke in the evening darkness, it was to hear the choking cry of the leopard beneath his very window. As he looked out, buckling on his scabbard, he saw a white shape slipping in and out of the shadows in the garden below. He took up his dagger in his hand and leaped over the threshold.

He had barely touched ground when, with a terrible snarl, the leopard bounded out of the obscurity of the hedged garden wall and came to a stop before him. It was huge—bigger than any leopard Zufik had seen or heard of—and its pelt gleamed like ivory. It leaped, claws flashing, and he could barely throw himself down in time as the beast passed over him like a cloud, touching him only with its hot breath. It turned and leaped again as the palace dogs set up a terrible barking, and this time its talons raked Zufik's chest, knocking him tumbling. Blood started from his shirt, spouting so fiercely that he could scarcely draw himself to his feet. He was caught with his back against the garden wall; the leopard slowly moved toward him, yellow eyes like tallow lamps burning in the niches of Hell.

Suddenly there was a crashing at the far end of the garden: The sultan's dogs had broken down their stall and were even now speeding through the trees. The leopard hesitated—Zufik could almost see it thinking—and then, with a last snarl, it leaped onto the wall and disappeared into the night.

Zufik was taken, his wounds bound, and he was put into his bed. The Princess Rassoril, who had truly lost her heart to him, wept bitterly at his side, begging him to go back to his father's land and to give up the fatal challenge. But Zufik, weak as he was, would no more think of yielding than he would of theft or treason, and refused, saying he would hunt the beast again the following night. Sifaz grinned and led the princess away. Zufik thought he heard the pale cousin whistling as he went.

In the dark before dawn Zufik, who could not sleep owing to the pain of his injury, heard his door quietly open. He was astonished to see the princess come in, gesturing him to silence. When the door was closed she threw herself down at his side and covered his hand and cheek with kisses, proclaiming her love for him and begging him again to flee. He admitted his love for her, but reminded her that his honor would not permit him to stop short of his goal, even should he die in the trying.

Rassoril, seeing that there was no changing the young prince's mind, took from her robe a black arrow tipped in silver, fletched with the tail feathers of a falcon. "Then take this," she said. "This leopard is a magic beast, and you will never kill it otherwise. Only silver will pierce its heart. Take the arrow and you may fulfill your oath." So saying, she slipped out of his room.

The next night Zufik again heard the leopard's voice in the garden below, but this time he took also his bow and arrow when he went out to meet it. At first he was loath to use it, since it seemed somehow unmanly; but when the beast had again given him injury and he had struck three sword blows in turn without effect, he at last nocked the silver-pointed shaft on his bowstring and, as the beast charged him once more, let fly. The black arrow struck to the leopard's heart; the creature gave a hideous cry and again leaped the fence, this time leaving a trail of its mortal blood behind it.

When morning came Zufik went to the sultan for men, so that they could follow the track of blood to the beast's lair and prove its death. The sultan was displeased when his vizier, the princess's pale cousin, did not answer his summons. As they were all going down into the garden, though, there came a great cry from the sleeping rooms upstairs, a cry like a soul in mortal agony. With fear in their hearts, Zufik, the sultan, and all the men rushed upstairs. There they found the missing Sifaz.

The pale man lifted a shaking, red-smeared finger to point at Zufik, as all the company stared in horror. "*He* has done it—the foreigner!" Sifaz shouted.

In Sifaz's arms lay the body of the Princess Rassoril, a black arrow standing from her breast.

After Fawn finished there was a long silence. The boy, his own courage perhaps stirred by his story, seemed to sit straighter.

"Ah . . ." the vampyr said at last, "love and its prices—that is the message? Or is it perhaps the effect of silver on the supernatural? Fear not, I am bound by no such conventions, and fear neither

silver, steel, nor any other metal." The creature made a huffing, scraping sound that might have been a laugh. I marveled anew, even as I felt the skein of my life fraying, that it had so quickly gained such command of our unfamiliar tongue.

"Well . . ." it said slowly. "Sad. But . . . sad enough? Again, *that* is the important question. What is your next . . . offering?"

I hunched to hide my shiver. For the creature, it was a game.

Ibrahim, who had watched Fawn attentively (as had Abdallah) while he told his tale, moved his shoulders and then winced. When the pain left his face, he stared at the vampyr.

"I believe I am ready," he said.

Chapter 15:
THE TALE OF IBRAHIM THE SLAVE

O strange and inscrutable creature [Ibrahim began] and comrades assembled, know that in the city of Cairo many years ago a most marvelous and terrible thing took place. There was living in that city a master of jewelcraft and blademaking, who took delight in the working of all metals with the aid of fire. The reek of hot metal was as the sweetest perfume to him. It was his delight to create for women ornaments to glorify the hair, forehead jewelry to accent the house of thought, rings to enliven the fingers, necklaces to embrace the throat and breast. It was said he could inscribe the name of Allah on the smallest link of the finest chain, so that whoever wore such a chain would be protected from the evil eye; and the moon-shaped pendants he made would protect their wearers even from death. His curved daggers were said to cry in their sheaths for blood, and his swords could cut through marble and not be dulled.

Because his work was so fine, his fame spread far and wide.

One day a stranger came into his shop and said, "Make for me a cane of the purest silver, but strong as Damascene steel, and decorated all over with stars and crescents and charms to ward off evil, and I will give you a thousand dinars. But first, let me take all this stuff in your shop away—for you have only inferior metals here. You must buy the finest silver in the market." And saying such, he carried away all of the smith's supplies.

The smith was excited by this commission, which would surely challenge his abilities to their limits, and by the promise of the fee, which was very great. Abandoning his other pursuits, he threw himself into crafting the perfect *asa,* cane, for this stranger. He went down to the market and bought the purest silver at the greatest cost and took it home to his shop. He poured into the making of the cane all his arcane secrets of metallurgy, all the craft of his hands, and all the blood of his heart; so that by the seventh day he had made a cane perfect to all specifications the stranger had given him. Looking upon what he had created, he said, "By Allah, it is surely the most wonderful thing ever I have made."

That evening the stranger stopped by, and the smith showed him the cane.

"This?" cried the stranger, snatching up the cane. "You call this a finished work?"

In a rage, the stranger lifted the cane and smashed it down against the smith's anvil, and with such great strength did he strike that the cane, made to crack rock, smashed in half, the pieces flying off. "I will have blood payment for this insult!" cried the stranger, and pulling out a golden dagger, he struck off the smith's little fingers on both hands.

"Now," he said, "you will make for me a phial fit to hold the finest kohl eye paint, eye paint which will strengthen the vision to the utmost and purify the eyes. This kohl-phial must be filigreed all over with threads as fine as maiden hair, shaped in the images of flowers such as grew in the hanging gardens of Babylon."

"But, Lord," protested the smith, "those gardens were built a thousand years ago, and have been gone almost that long. How am I to know which flowers bloomed there?"

"You will accept my commission, and remember that my dagger is hungry," said the stranger. And he left the forge.

The smith stared at his greatest work in pieces

at his feet, and at his hands, now bereft of their smallest fingers. He bound his wounds. His heart sickened within him, for he did not know how he could work with such pain in his hands, but not to work for the terrible stranger could mean something even worse. For a little while he thought of packing up his belongings, wives, children, and household treasures, and leaving Cairo; with his skills, he and his family would doubtless be welcome anywhere. But something there was about the dark stranger that told him there would be no escaping.

And so he set to work.

Seven days and nights he worked to pull silver into thinnest thread, to fashion thread into fairest flowers, to shape flowers around a kohl-phial of finest beaten silver, with a bodkin to fit in the stopper, the outer end shaped after the manner of foliage. In the midst of his work, he forgot his pain, for the work became meat and drink to him, shelter and warmth; and when at last he polished off the last of working tarnish from the piece, he was satisfied that it was the finest thing he had ever made.

That evening, in came the stranger, and cried, "Where is my kohl-phial?"

Though he knew in his heart that this kohl-phial was a fine and a perfect piece of work, still the smith's hand trembled when he offered it to the stranger.

For a moment the stranger studied the kohl-phial, turning it over in his hand tenderly, as if he too saw its worth. For a moment the smith dared to hope. But then the stranger cast the fine fili-greed phial to the ground and cried in great rage, "What is this!?" He stamped down his boot upon the phial, crushing it utterly. "You insult me with this inferior filth!"

The smith cried aloud to see such beauty destroyed, and the stranger advanced toward him. Pulling out his golden dagger, the stranger seized the smith's hands and sliced off his thumbs.

"Now," he said, "you will make for me a dagger that stays sharp no matter what I use it for, even to cut diamond; and you will gift it with a small piece of your soul, to keep it true. And, because this earthly forge-fire is impure, I will take it from you. You must ask heaven for a purer flame." So saying, he left the smith, and the fire went out as he departed.

In the darkness left behind, the smith bound his wounds, and knew at last that the stranger had given him an impossible charge. He knew of no metal that would keep an edge in the face of diamond; he knew of no way to sever a piece of his soul and put it into metal (though perhaps he had done it already in crafting the kohl-phial and the cane), and he knew of no way to work metal and temper it without fire. Even when he called his son in to make up a fire, no fire would come to his forge. So he sat in the ruins of his career, bereft of thumbs and thus of dexterity to work with his tools. For a period he gave way to despair; and at last he closed his shop and set his family to begging by the Gate of Victory.

This, it happened, was extremely pleasing to the smith who ran the shop next door to the first smith's shop, who because his own work was inferior had been losing business to him steadily. So this second smith had hired a Western magician to set an Ifrit on his rival, and did not care if the ruin came at the cost of an entire life's dreams broken beneath the heel of a horrifying, devilish, and insatiable creature. . . .

Ibrahim's voice trailed off, and he gripped his useless arm with his good hand. I could almost grasp what it meant to the smith to lose his ability to pursue his craft; but it was something *I* did not wish to know.

The vampyr turned his face away from the fire, so that his red eyes were not visible for a moment. He stared at the ground. Then he looked up. "Sad, perhaps. I am not certain of the lesson. Sad enough? You shall judge. Who speaks next?"

Now my heart truly went cold within me, and I sat as though I had swallowed a stone. Walid al-Salameh spoke up.

"I do," he said, and took a deep breath. "I do."

Chapter 16:
THE TALE OF
THE UNDER-VIZIER
WALID AL-SALAMEH

This is a true story [the Under-Vizier commenced]—or so I was told. It happened in my grandfather's time, and he had it from someone who knew those involved. He told it to me as a cautionary tale.

There once was an old emir, a man of rare gifts and good fortune. He ruled a small country, but a wealthy one—a country upon which all the gifts of Allah had been showered in grand measure. He had the finest heir a man could have, dutiful and yet courageous, beloved by the people almost as extravagantly as the emir himself. He had many other fine sons, and two hundred beautiful wives, and an army of fighting men the envy of his neighbors. His treasury was stacked roofbeam-high with gold and gemstones and blocks of fragrant sandalwood, crisscrossed with ivories and bolts of the finest cloth. His palace was built around a spring of fragrant, clear water, and everyone said that they must be the very Waters of Life, so fortunate and well-loved this emir was. His only sadness was that age had robbed his sight from him, leaving him blind, but hard as this was, it was a small price to pay for Allah's beneficence.

One day the emir was walking in his garden, smelling the exquisite fragrance of the blossoming orange trees. His son the prince, unaware of his father's presence, was also in the garden, conversing with his mother, the emir's first and chiefest wife.

"He is terribly old," the wife said. "I cannot stand even to touch him anymore. It is a horror to me."

"You are right, mother," the son replied, as the emir hid behind the trees and listened, shocked. "I am sickened by watching him sitting all day, drooling into his bowl, or staggering sightless through the palace. But what are we to do?"

"I have thought on it long and hard," the emir's wife replied. "We owe it to ourselves and those close to us to kill him."

"Kill him?" the son replied. "Well, it is hard for me, but I suppose you are right. I still feel

some love for him, though—may we at least do it quickly, so that he shall not feel pain at the end?"

"Very well. But do it soon—tonight, even. If I must feel his foul breath upon me one more night I will die myself."

"Tonight, then," the son agreed, and the two walked away, leaving the blind emir shaking with rage and terror behind the orange trees. He could not see what sat on the garden path behind them, the object of their discussion: the wife's old lapdog, a scrofulous creature of extreme age.

Thus the emir went to his vizier, the only one he was sure he could trust in a world of suddenly traitorous sons and wives, and bade him to have the pair arrested and quickly beheaded. The vizier was shocked, and asked the reason why, but the emir only said he had unassailable proof that they intended to murder him and take his throne. He bade the vizier go and do the deed.

The vizier did as he was directed, seizing the son and his mother quickly and quietly, then giving them over to the headsman after tormenting them for confessions and the names of confederates, neither of which were forthcoming.

Sadly, the vizier went to the emir and told him it was done, and the old man was satisfied. But soon, inevitably, word of what had happened spread, and the brothers of the heir began to murmur among themselves about their father's deed.

Many thought him mad, since the dead pair's devotion to the emir was common knowledge.

Word of this dissension reached the emir himself, and he began to fear for his life, terrified that his other sons meant to emulate their treasonous brother. He called the vizier to him and demanded the arrest of these sons, and their beheading. The vizier argued in vain, risking his own life, but the emir would not be swayed; at last the vizier went away. He returned a week later a battered, shaken man.

"It is done, O Prince," he said. "All your sons are dead."

The emir had only a short while in which to feel safe before the extreme wrath of the wives over the slaughter of their children reached his ears. "Destroy them, too!" the blind emir insisted.

Again the vizier went away, soon to return.

"It is done, O Prince," he reported. "Your wives have been beheaded."

Soon the courtiers were crying murder, and the emir sent his vizier to see them dealt with as well.

"It is done, O Prince," he assured the emir a fortnight later. But the ruler now feared the angry townspeople, so he commanded his vizier to take the army and slaughter them. The vizier argued feebly, then went away.

"It is done, O Prince," the emir was told after a month had passed. But now the emir realized

that with his heirs and wives gone, and the important men of the court dead, it was the soldiers
themselves who were a threat to his power. He
commanded his vizier to sow lies amongst them,
causing them to fall out and slay each other, then
locked himself in his room to safely outlast the
conflict. After a month and a half the vizier
knocked upon his door.

"It is done, O Prince."

For a moment the emir was satisfied. All his
enemies were dead, and he himself was locked in:
No one could murder him, or steal his treasure,
or usurp his throne. The only person yet alive who
even knew where the emir hid was . . . his vizier.

Blind, he groped about for the key with
which he had locked himself in. Better first to re-
move the risk that someone might trick him into
coming out. He pushed the key out beneath the
door and told the vizier to throw it away somewhere it might never be found. When the vizier
returned he called him close to the locked portal
that bounded his small world of darkness and
safety.

"Vizier," the emir said through the keyhole,
"I command you to go and kill yourself, for you
are the last one living who is a threat to me."

"*Kill* myself, my prince?" the vizier asked,
dumbfounded. "Kill *myself*?"

"Correct," the emir said. "Now go and do
it. That is my command."

There was a long silence. At last the vizier said: "Very well." After that there was silence.

For a long time the emir sat in his blindness and exulted, for everyone he distrusted was gone. His faithful vizier had carried out all his orders, and now had killed himself. . . .

A sudden horrible thought came to him then: What if the vizier had *not* done what he had told him to do? What if instead he had made a compact with the emir's enemies, and was only reporting false details when he told of their deaths? How was the emir to know?

He almost swooned with fright and anxiety at the realization.

At last he worked up the courage to feel his way across the locked room to the door. He put his ear to the keyhole and listened. He heard nothing but silence. He took a breath and then put his mouth to the hole.

"Vizier?" he called in a shaky voice. "Have you done what I commanded? Have you killed yourself?"

"It is done, O Prince," came the reply.

Finishing his story, which was fully as dreadful as it was sad, the Under-Vizier Walid lowered his head as if ashamed or exhausted.

Ibn Fahad cast fresh wood on the fire, though its light did not drive away our unwelcome guest. The thought of warmth was comforting, and yet when I stretched out my hands to the fire, the chill in my heart did not thaw. I did not know if the Vizier's story might succeed if the others failed; and I did know that it was at last my turn to tell a tale.

So, despite the tatters worn in my story-telling abilities by our last ten days, despite the weariness I felt from lack of sleep, it was time for me to make my own feeble attempt.

(Yes, yes, Ibn Fahad, well may you smile. You are right; I have never held my abilities in low esteem. I indeed thought it might be my tale that would save our lives, and so I could not leave it unsaid.)

When the creature cast its ruby gaze upon me, I took a sip of water to cleanse my mouth, and began.

Chapter 17:
MASRUR'S TALE

In ages gone and times forgotten [I began], there lived a young man who had spent all his life in abject poverty. He labored for others, serving in the lowliest positions, begging from beggars, a slave to slaves. Withal, he walked the streets with a bright eye, happy on the days when Fortune granted him a pinch of spice for his rice or the rind of a pomegranate with a few seeds still clinging to it, yet always looking for an opportunity to better his condition and himself.

It so chanced one day that a rich lady, her eyes beautiful as night above a veil hung all over with moons of silver, the ankle-bands of her trousers laced with tiny bells that made her walk a thing of music, stopped beside the young man in the marketplace, where he sat with a crate he had scavenged from a midden.

The rich woman said, "Bring your crate and follow me."

The young man rose immediately, thanking Allah for this providence; surely a woman laced with silver, carrying a heavy purse (for he could see the weight of it as it swayed against the inside of her cloak), with rich smells making all pure around her, jasmine drifting from her hidden hair, rose and aloewood beautifying her clothes, surely a woman such as this would give him a fine payment when he had done her bidding.

She led him through the city to the door of a shop and bade him stay outside. An old man with a patch over one eye answered her knock and they both stepped inside the shop for a moment. They were not out of the young man's sight, but what passed between them he could not see, for they had their backs to him. When the woman emerged a moment later, she handed to the young man a package wrapped in white silk.

"Put this in your crate and follow," she said.

He followed her as she led him through the streets on the strangest journey he had yet taken. They passed through gates that he did not see until she opened them, crossed deserted courtyards with strange symbols painted on the walls, and walked in and out of narrow streets and shadowed alleys he had never suspected existed, although he had been in and about the city all his life and thought he knew every byway.

At last she came to a red door and stopped. A slave answered her summons and fell back before her, lowering his head.

"Come," she said to the young man, who followed her inside, where he discovered such luxuries as he had never even heard stories of, such wonders as beggared dreams. From the rich colors of the hangings, the tiled floors that gleamed in the few spaces not covered by carpets of the finest weave, the peacock feathers standing in vases, the smell of fine food and rich incense, to the very softness of the air, it was nearly too much for him. It was all so beautiful he wanted to run away. Somewhere not far away he heard the sound water makes in a gentle fountain; from another direction came the soft murmurs of captive birds. He thought he was in Paradise.

"Set down your burden," said the woman.

Gently he pulled the silken package from his crate and set it upon the floor. Through the white silk he felt something hard, with square angles, and it bore the tang of metal. It was warmer under his hand than its brief journey beneath the sun merited. He suddenly wanted very much to know what it was that he had carried across the city. He released the package and looked up at the woman.

"Here is a dinar for your trouble," she said, handing him a gold piece, and she nodded to the slave to show him out.

For a moment he stood staring at her, then the slave touched his arm. But the woman lifted a hand to stay the slave.

"The young man is right," she said. "This is a poor reward for his service. Let us feed him before sending him out again," she said. He could not see her veiled mouth, but he knew from her eyes that she smiled, and in that moment a longing was born in his chest, a restlessness like that of a falcon unhooded after hours in darkness.

The slave left the room and presently returned with a plaited palm-mat, which he set on the floor. "Be seated," said the woman, and the young man sat, and then she offered him the most beautiful selection of fruits, sweets, nuts, and coffee, and more, so much more. . . .

The young man, who had eaten many things in his life, things that no civilized man would touch, that night felt he had tasted the foods of Heaven and seen the shape of one who might serve in the blessed Garden. Yet all the time, not far away lay the package wrapped in its shroud of silk.

At last he finished his meal. This time when the slave led him back toward the door he had no reason to resist, except for the curiosity and longing that consumed him, and these were not proper

reasons. He thanked the lady and her slave for their hospitality, and went out into the night.

Not long thereafter he was constrained to join the army, and after some years of serving his Caliph, he was forced to march far from his native land, driven to sleep beneath wet, forbidding skies among cold mountains, threatened with an awful death, and finally forced to fight for his miserable life with stories . . . with words.

Still, the mysteries of the package and the woman remain. Through all that has beset me since that long-ago night—for, of course, that young man was I—I have never been able to guess what lay within that white silk or what lay behind that silver-strung veil. And if death in these haunted mountains prevents my return to my native land, where I might otherwise someday find the answer to these questions, it is a mystery that will surely gnaw at my soul until the last trumpet of eternity, even should I—unlikely thought!—be welcomed into the real Paradise. Saddest of all sadnesses, I think: never to know.

It was silent around the campfire when I finished. I was afraid that, after all, my tale was weakest.

We waited tensely for our guest to speak; at the same time I am sure we all vainly hoped there would be no more speaking, that the creature would simply vanish, like a frightening dream that flees the sun.

"Rather than discuss the merits of your sad tales," the black, tattered shadow said at last—confirming that there would be no waking from this dream—"rather than argue the game with only one set of moves completed, perhaps it is now time for me to speak. The night is still youthful, and my tale is not long, but I wish to give you a fair time to render judgment."

As he spoke the creature's eyes bloomed scarlet like unfolding roses. The mist curled up from the ground beyond the fire-circle, wrapping the vampyr in a cloak of writhing fogs, a rotted black egg in a bag of silken mesh.

"May I begin. . . ?" the thing asked. No one could say a word. "Very well . . ."

Chapter 18:

THE TALE OF THE VAMPYR

The tale I tell is of a child [the vampyr intoned], a child born in an ancient city on the banks of a river.

So long ago this was that not only has the city itself long gone to dust; but the later cities built atop its ruins—tiny towns and great walled fortresses of stone—all these too have gone beneath the millwheels of time—rendered, like their predecessor, into the finest of particles to blow in the wind, silting the timeless river's banks.

This child lived in a mud hut thatched with reeds, and played with his fellows in the shallows of the sluggish brown river while his mother washed the family's clothes and gossiped with her neighbors.

Even *this* ancient city was built upon the

bones of earlier cities, and it was into the collapsed remnants of one—a great, tumbled mass of shattered sandstone—that the child and his friends sometimes went. And it was to these ruins that the child, when he was a little older . . . almost the age of your young, romantic companion . . . took a pretty, doe-eyed girl.

It was to be his first time beyond the veil— his initiation into the mysteries of women. His heart beat rapidly as he watched the girl walk ahead of him, her slender brown body tiger-striped with light and shade as she passed among the broken pillars. Then she saw something, and screamed. The child came running.

The girl was nearly mad, weeping and pointing. The child stopped in amazement, staring at the black, shrivelled thing that lay on the ground—a twisted something that might have been a man once, wizened and black as a piece of leather dropped into the cookfire. Then the thing opened its eyes.

The girl ran, choking . . . but he did not, seeing that surely the black thing could not move. The twitching of its mouth seemed that of someone trying to speak; he thought he heard a faint voice asking for help, begging for him to do something. He leaned down to the near-silent hiss, and the thing squirmed and bit him, fastening its sharp teeth like barbed fish-hooks into the muscle of his leg.

The man-child screamed, helpless, and felt his blood running out into the horrible sucking mouth of the thing. Fetid saliva crept into the wounds and coursed hotly through his body, even as he struggled against his writhing attacker. The poison climbed through him, and it seemed he could feel his own heart flutter and die within his chest, delicate and hopeless as a broken bird. With final, desperate strength the child pulled free. The black thing, mouth gaping, curled on itself and shuddered like a beetle on a hot stone. A moment later it had crumbled into ashes and oily flakes.

But it had caught me long enough to destroy me—for *I* was that child—to force its foul fluids into me, leeching my humanity and replacing it with the hideous, unwanted wine of immortality. My child's heart became an icy fist.

Thus was I made what I am at the hands of a dying vampyr, which had been a creature like I am now. Worn down at last by the passing of millennia, it had chosen a host to receive its hideous malady, then died—as I shall do too someday, no doubt, in the grip of some terrible, blind, insectlike urge . . . but not soon. Not today.

So that child, which had been in all ways like other children—loved by its family, loving in turn noise and games and sweetmeats—became a dark thing sickened by the burning light of the sun.

Driven into the damp shadows beneath stones and the dusty gloom of abandoned places, then

driven out again beneath the moon by an unshak-
able, irresistible hunger, I fed first on my family—
my uncomprehending mother wept to see her
child returned, standing by her moonlit pallet—
then on the others of my city. Not last or least
painful of my feedings was on the dark-haired girl
who had run when I stayed behind. I slashed other
throats too and sucked out salty, life-hot blood
while the trapped child inside me cried without a
sound. It was as though I stood behind a screen,
unable to leave or interfere as terrible crimes were
committed before me. . . .

And thus the years have passed: sand grains,
deposited along the river bank, uncountable in
their succession. Every one has contained a seeming infinitude of killings, each one terrible despite
their numbing similarity. Only the blood of man-
kind will properly feed me, and a hundred genera-
tions have known the terror of me.

Strong as I am, virtually immortal, unkillable
as far as I know or can tell—blades pass through
me like smoke; fire, water, poison, none affect
me—still the light of the sun causes a pain to me
so excruciating that you with only mortal lives,
whose pain at least eventually ends in death, cannot possibly comprehend it. Thus, kingdoms of
men have risen and fallen to ashes since I last saw
daylight. Think only on that for a moment, if you
seek sad stories! I must be in darkness when the
sun rises, so as I range in search of prey my ac-

commodations are shared with toads and slugs, bats and worms.

People can be nothing to me anymore but food. I know of no other like myself, save the dying creature who spawned me. The smell of my own corruption is in my nostrils always.

So there is all of *my* tale. I cannot die until my time is come, and who can know when that is? Until then I will be alone, alone as no mere man can ever be, alone with my wretchedness and meaningless evil and self-disgust until the world collapses and is born anew. . . .

The vampyr rose now, towering like a black sail billowing in the wind, spreading its vast arms or wings on either side, as if to sweep us before it.

"How do your stories compare to this?" it cried. The harshness of its speech seemed somehow muted, even as it grew louder and louder. "Whose is the saddest story, then?" There was pain in that hideous voice that tore at even my fast-pounding heart. "Whose is saddest? Tell me! It is time to *judge* . . ."

And in that moment, of all the moments when lying could save my life . . . I could not lie. I turned my face away from the quivering black shadow, that thing of rags and red eyes. None of the others around the campfire spoke—even Abdallah the clerk only sat hugging his knees, teeth chattering, eyes bulging with fear.

". . . I thought so," the thing said at last. "I thought so."

Night wind tossed the tree limbs above our heads, and it seemed as though beyond them stood only ultimate darkness—no sky, no stars, nothing but unending emptiness.

"Very well," the vampyr said at last. "Your silence speaks all. I have won." There was not the slightest note of triumph in its voice. "Give me my prize, and then I might let the rest of you flee my mountains." The dark shape withdrew a little way.

We all of us turned to look at one another, and it was just as well that the night veiled our faces. I started to speak, but Ibn Fahad interrupted me, his voice a tortured rasp.

"Let there be no talk of volunteering. We will draw lots; that is the only way." Quickly he cut a thin branch into eight pieces, one of them shorter than the rest, and cupped them in a closed hand.

"Pick," he said. "I will keep the last."

As a part of me wondered what madness it was that had left us wagering on storytelling and drawing lots for our lives, we each took a length from Ibn Fahad's fist. I kept my hand closed while the others selected, not wanting to hurry Allah toward His revelation of my fate. When all had

131

selected we extended our hands and opened them, palms up.

Young Fawn had selected the short stick.

Strangely, there was no sign of his awful fortune on his face. He showed no signs of grief—indeed, he did not even respond to our helpless words and prayers, only stood up and slowly walked toward the huddled black shape at the far edge of the clearing. The vampyr rose to meet him.

"No!" came a sudden cry, and to our complete surprise the clerk Abdallah leaped to his feet and went pelting across the open space, throwing himself between the youth and the looming shadow. "He is too young, too perfect!" Abdallah shouted, sounding truly anguished. "Do not do this terrible thing! Take me instead!"

The rest of us could only sit, struck dumb by this unexpected behavior, but the creature moved swiftly as a viper, smacking Abdallah to the ground with one flicking gesture.

"You are indeed mad, you short-lived men!" the vampyr hissed. "This one would do nothing to save himself—not once did I hear his voice raised in tale-telling—yet now he would throw himself into the jaws of death for this other! Mad!"

The monster left Abdallah choking on the ground and turned to silent Fawn.

"Come you. I have won the contest, and you are the prize. I am . . . sorry . . . it must be this way . . ." A great swath of darkness enveloped the youth, drawing him in. "Come," the vampyr said, "think of the better world you go to—that is what you believe, is it not? Well, soon you shall . . ."

The creature broke off.

"Why do you look so strangely, man-child?" the thing said at last, its voice troubled. "You cry, but I see no fear. Why? Are you not afraid of dying?"

Fawn answered; his tones were oddly distracted. "Have you really lived so long? And alone, always alone?"

"I told you. I have no reason to lie. Do you think to put me off with your strange questions?"

"Ah, how could the good God be so unmerciful?" Fawn murmured. His words were made of sighs. The dark shape that embraced him stiffened.

"Do you cry for *me? For me?!*"

"How can I help?" the boy said. "Even Allah must weep for you . . . for such a pitiful thing, lost in the lonely darkness . . ."

For a moment the night air seemed to pulse. Then, with a wrenching gasp, the creature flung Fawn backward so that the youth stumbled and fell before us, landing atop the groaning Abdallah.

"*Go!*" the vampyr shrieked, and its voice cracked and boomed like thunder—yet somehow I thought I heard weeping in it. "Get you gone from my mountains! *Go!*"

Amazed, we pulled Fawn and the chief clerk to their feet and went stumbling down the hillside, branches lashing at our faces and hands, expecting any moment to hear the rush of wings and feel cold breath on our necks.

"Build your houses well, little men!" a voice howled like the wild wind behind us. "My life is long . . . and someday I may regret letting you go!"

We ran and ran, dragging each other, half-carrying Ibrahim, until it seemed the life would flee our bodies, until our lungs burned and our feet blistered . . . and until the topmost sliver of the sun peered over the eastern summits.

EPILOGUE

Masrur al-Adan allowed the tale's ending to hang in silence for a span of thirty heartbeats, then pushed his chair away from the table.

"We escaped the mountains the next day," he said. "Within a season we were back in Baghdad, the only survivors of the caravan to the Armenites."

"Aaaahh . . . !" breathed young Hassan, a long drawn-out sound full of wonder and apprehension. "What a marvelous, terrifying adventure! I would *never* have survived it, myself. How frightening! What became of all your fellow adventurers?"

Masrur stroked his beard and smiled.

Ibn Fahad snorted, awake after all. "The only

time his tongue fails him is in discussion of his few redeeming qualities," he said. "Old Ibrahim, aided by the Armenite woman Sossi, is master of Masrur's kitchen; I am sure your stomachs agree that he has a way with pigeons. The young man Kurken became the stablemaster, and both he and Sossi have grown, if not old, at least plump and comfortable in Masrur's service. Those two could never have married had they returned to their homes.

"And the rest of the caravan survivors . . ." he negligently waved his hand, ". . . are scattered to the winds."

"Marvelous!" said Hassan. "And did the . . . the creature . . . did he *really* say he might come back someday?"

Masrur solemnly nodded his large head. "Upon my soul. Am I not right, Ibn Fahad, my old comrade?"

Ibn Fahad yielded a thin smile, seemingly of affirmation.

"Yes," Masrur continued, "those words chill me to this very day. Many is the night I have sat in this room, looking at that door—" he pointed— "wondering if someday it might open to reveal that terrible, misshapen black thing, come back from Hell to make good on our wager."

"Merciful Allah!" Hassan gasped.

Abu Jamir leaned across the tale as the other guests whispered excitedly. He wore a look of annoyance. "Good Hassan," he snapped, "kindly calm yourself. We are all grateful to our host Masrur for entertaining us, but it is an insult to sensible, Godly men to suggest that at any moment some blood-drinking ifrit may knock down the door and carry us—"

At that instant the door leaped open with a crash, revealing a hideous, twisted shape looming in the entrance, red-splattered and trembling. The shrieking of Masrur's guests filled the room.

"Master . . . ?" the dark silhouette quavered. Old Baba held a wine jar balanced on one shoulder. The other had broken at the servant's feet, splashing Abu Jamir's prize stock everywhere. "Master," Baba began again, "I am afraid I have dropped one."

Masrur looked down at Abu Jamir, who had fainted and lay pitched full-length on the floor.

"Ah, well, that's all right, Baba." Masrur smiled, twirling his black mustache. "We won't have to make the wine go so far as I thought—it seems my storytelling has put some of our guests to sleep."